THE GIRL IN THE GRAVE

A JIMMY RILEY NOIR NOVEL

MICHAEL LISTER

Print ISBN: 978-1-947606-07-4

The Girl in the Grave, the 2nd Jimmy Riley Noir Novel, was originally published as The Big Beyond.

Join Michael's Readers' Group and receive 4 FREE Books!

Books by Michael Lister

Sign up for Michael's newsletter by clicking here or go to www.MichaelLister.com and receive a free book.

(Jimmy Riley Novels)
The Girl Who Said Goodbye
The Girl in the Grave
The Girl at the End of the Long Dark Night
The Girl Who Cried Blood Tears
The Girl Who Blew Up the World

(John Jordan Novels)
Power in the Blood
Blood of the Lamb
Flesh and Blood
(Special Introduction by Margaret Coel)
The Body and the Blood

Double Exposure
Blood Sacrifice
Rivers to Blood
Burnt Offerings
Innocent Blood
(Special Introduction by Michael Connelly)
Separation Anxiety
Blood Money Blood Moon
Thunder Beach
Blood Cries
A Certain Retribution
Blood Oath
Blood Work
Cold Blood
Blood Betrayal
Blood Shot
Blood Ties
Blood Stone
Blood Trail

(Merrick McKnight / Reggie Summers Novels)
Thunder Beach
A Certain Retribution
Blood Oath
Blood Shot

(Remington James Novels)
Double Exposure
(includes intro by Michael Connelly)
Separation Anxiety
Blood Shot

(Sam Michaels / Daniel Davis Novels)
Burnt Offerings
Blood Oath
Cold Blood
Blood Shot

(Love Stories)

Carrie's Gift

(Short Story Collections)
North Florida Noir
Florida Heat Wave
Delta Blues
Another Quiet Night in Desperation

(The Meaning Series)
Meaning Every Moment
The Meaning of Life in Movies

THE GIRL IN THE GRAVE

1

When they came to kill me, I was in no condition to defend myself.

This would've presented more of a dilemma had I not wanted to die.

For days doctors and nurses had done everything they could to keep me alive—everything but the one thing that would've made me want to live.

They hadn't kept her from dying.

No, that was no good. That's the story I kept trying to sell myself, but I wasn't buying.

The unimaginably ugly truth—the one I had no defenses for —was this: They didn't let her die. I did.

No, that's no good either.

I didn't just let her die. I killed her.

Days in a drug-addled delirium had done little to diminish that devastating fact.

In my morphine-induced disintegration, I was drowning in a dark ocean, breaking the surface of the swells only occasionally to recall a random rivulet of conversation or glimpse the distorted reflection of her in an oblique object.

I remembered I had told her I could save her.

"All right, soldier," she had said. "See what you can do. I don't mind."

I had believed I could, thought I might somehow undo the damage I had already done.

Memories little more than mist. Fragile evanescent fragments.

Passion and obsession bordering on madness. When we were together, nothing else in the world seemed to matter—there didn't seem to be anything else in the world.

Whiling away the time like lovers do, like it could never be exhausted.

Lying in between sand dunes looking up at the stars, listening to the unseen waves of the Gulf caress the shore. Beneath us, the sand soft and cool, above us, the sky dark and clear and dotted with stars, and around us, the beach empty for miles.

"Listen, soldier. This is the big love for me. I'll never love another man. Not ever. This won't end for me—even if you end it. I'll still love you the way I've never loved anyone in my whole entire life."

DOA.

I didn't know that I hadn't saved her until days after I had failed to do so.

I had no memory of crashing my car into the main entrance of Johnston's Sanatorium or the doctor's pronouncement that she was dead on arrival.

While she was sleeping the big sleep, I was trapped in a deep well between daylight and darkness, between death and the half life I would have without her if I was able to claw my way out of it and not wake up only to eat my revolver.

But coming out of the coma hadn't ended the purgatorial plane of my empty existence. I was just awake for it now.

Adrift.

Untethered.

Weightless.

One moment I was floating through the zero gravity black void of an empty, silent hell, the next I was bobbing like a buoy in the bay between consciousness and unconsciousness, between the bad dreams of sleep and the waking nightmare that was now my existence entire.

I had just surfaced when they showed up.

I had no idea who sent them, but whoever hired the menacing muscle here to break the spring of my mortal coil had spared no expense. Even if I wasn't weak and wounded from being gut shot, even if I cared anything at all about living a life without Lauren in it, even if I wasn't a right-handed man with only his left, I wasn't sure I could've prevented them from putting the big pinch on me––but as it was there was nothing I could do but lie there and watch my fate unfold.

Both guys were big and broad and hard, but the bigger of the two stood watch at the door while the other, dressed in an ill-fitting white coat, came inside.

"Hey, Doc," I said, "your coat don't fit so good."

"Yeah? Well, there's a war on, or haven't you heard?"

"Yeah I heard."

The too small lab coat covered a darby drape and foreign kicks that looked to have cost plenty of lettuce.

"So what's my prognosis?" I asked. "Worse now I bet."

He smiled. "A wise guy, huh?"

"Not wise enough. Not by a mile."

"What are you going on about, mister?"

"Just saying I know you."

"I don't think so."

"Well, I know your kind. Know why you're here."

"Then you know how this is gotta go, soldier."

"I do. And I don't mind so much."

"On account of the dame?"

"Just tell me who's punchin' my ticket."

"Can't do that."

"Nothing to lose, mister. Why not spill? No one'll ever know."

"Sorry, soldier. It's just not in the cards."

"Don't seem so much to ask. Be a pal and grant a dying man his last wish."

He pulled a syringe out of his coat pocket.

"You're not fading so fast partner," he said, plunging the needle into the side of my neck. "We were told to hurt you some first."

2

I woke up in a dim dungeon-like room, strapped spread-eagle to a metal barrack-style bunk, a bright bare bulb hanging above me.

I was naked, hungry, and in excruciating pain.

The carnage that was my upper torso looked even more dramatic beneath the direct light—the short stump of right arm, the old scatter of shotgun wounds that had cost me the limb the year before, the fresh bloody mess of gut shot wound in my abdomen and the seeping bandages partially covering it, the various bruises, cuts, and scrapes dotting the pale, overexposed battleground that was my body—but nothing made me feel more helpless, more exposed, more embarrassed than my flaccid phallus lying limply on the dark patch of pubic hair.

I couldn't see much beyond the circle of light I was in the center of, but I was pretty sure the medical-looking machines were torture devices.

A pungent chemical smell permeated the air, but I couldn't place it. From an unseen sink somewhere close by, a leaking tap dripped an irritating, incessant wet thumph.

Thumph.

Thumph.

Thumph.

A tall, thin blonde woman in a lab coat came into the room, her heels, at least one of them in need of repair, clicking on the bare cement floor beneath her. Her fine hair was short, her bangs jagged, her ice blue eyes bits of frozen pond water beneath razor-thin, severely arching eyebrows.

"And how are ve today?" she asked as she reached the side of my bed.

"Well, I can't speak for you 'cause we just met, but I'mdandy as hell."

"Zis means . . . you are vhat?"

Her accent was vaguely European, but I couldn't say much beyond that––and I got the impression that she was maybe even faking it or at least exaggerating it a bit for my benefit. "Pardon?"

"Vhat means dandy?"

"Good. Jake. A-okay. Dillinger. Fine. Spiffy. Darby. Great. Wonderful. Never been better."

"Really? Is zis attempt at humor?"

"Sister, when I attempt humor you'll know it."

"I zank you are not being completely honest with Christa. I zank you are veak and can use some zing."

"Somezing like what?" I asked.

"No. Not somezing. Some zing. Some boost. Energy. Jolt. A pick-up you."

"A pick-up me?"

"Yes."

As she said this she turned away for a moment and grabbed something I couldn't see. When she turned back around, she was holding clamps attached to electrical cords––as if a smaller version of automotive starter cables.

"Why don't you hook yourself up to those things and see if you can jump-start your heart?" I asked.

"Zese are for you."

"I feel bad," I said. "I didn't get you anything."

"Let's see . . . vere should ve attach zese?"

She trailed the cold metal clamp across my chest, grazing my nipples, then down the length of my body to my flaccid penis.

"Yes. Here vill do just fine. Zis could use some pick-up, no?"

"No."

"Yeah sure."

"No offense, lady, but there's nothing you have that can get a rise out of me."

She attached one clamp to the tip of my penis and the other to the base of the shaft.

"Ve shall see. Zis should do it, no?"

"Haven't seen anyzing else in ze room zat could."

"You mock me, no?"

"I mock you, yes."

"I like zat. I am getting very vet."

Unlike her words, her face showed no reaction to either the insult or the mockery. It was as if it was a mask, a facade incapable of expression. Without saying anything else, she turned and flipped a switch somewhere behind her, which was followed by a whir and high-pitched whine of a motor coming to life and warming up.

"Are you hungry?" she asked, her voice softer, lighter.

I didn't respond.

"You look hungry."

I wasn't hungry. I was famished. Starving. Desperate for some kind of sustenance. Crazed with the wanting of it.

I was cold too, shivering in my nakedness.

"Did you know zat ze Japanese eat zeir prisoners of var?" she asked. "Zey say it is because of Allied attacks on zeir supply lines, zat zey are dying from starvation, but zat is not it."

I had heard reports of Japanese beheading Allied pilots and cutting off flesh from their arms, legs, hips, and buttocks to fry up and eat. You never knew how much of that kind of thing was propaganda––or from which side it came––but I knew there was something to it. A buddy of mine who'd escaped a POW camp told me he'd witnessed it for himself.

"Zey do it, like everyone else, for power and terror."

She waited, but I didn't respond.

"Eating one's enemy is ze ultimate in taking his power, no? And him knowing you are going to do it puts within him ze ultimate terror."

She paused expectantly again, but I remained implacable.

"You doubt ze truth of my claim," she said. "Okay. Let's put it to ze test. Know zis, Mr. Riley. Vhen ve finish torturing you, my comrades and I are going to eat you."

There was a seismic shift in my shivering that had absolutely nothing to do with the cold.

"We are going to remove choice cuts of ze flesh from your body while you are still alive and cook zem and eat zem. And you will be so starving, I will watch as you eat your own flesh. You will know ze true terror from zis moment and I will have all your power, no?"

3

She went at me hard—never changing her expression, no matter how painful for me or distasteful for her the tortuous task was.

The electrical current she continually administered to my genitalia and other parts of my body was not only extremely painful, but gave me the most unnatural sensation, which was nearly as bad as the burns and jolts.

As if the pain and distress weren't enough, the procedure caused me to lose control of both bladder and bowels, leaving me to writhe in my own waste.

I was glad she wasn't trying to break me, that I didn't have some important secret she was attempting to extract, for I would have long since told her anything she wanted to know.

When she had done her best, which was plenty, she left and the big man from the sanatorium came in.

"Whatta you think of her, soldier?"

"That's a waste of a woman," I said.

"Brother, you don't know the half of it."

"I know plenty. I promise you that."

"So I guess it's my turn," he said. "You ready?"

"Not really. No."

"What'd you do?"

"When?"

"What could you have possibly done to deserve all this," he said.

"Nobody deserves all this."

"What'd you do?"

"To who?"

"Really? You don't know? How many enemies capable of this you got?"

"Before tonight would've said none. Always thought I was beloved by all."

When I woke up, the big man was saying something.

"What?" I asked, my hoarse wisp of a voice not recognizable to me.

"How'd you lose the limb?"

"Found myself in a fight without a weapon," I said.

He nodded.

"So I chewed it off and clubbed the guy to death with it."

He laughed heartily at that.

"Thinking I'll do the same to you with the other one."

"You're all right, pal," he said. "You're all right."

"Yeah, I'm swell," I said. "Beloved by all."

"Tell you what, I'm gonna give you something. Knock you out so you won't be awake for the next round."

Before I could respond, he was administering an injection and I was slipping away.

The quality and quantity of light in the room changed and suddenly Lauren was standing beside my bed. She was luminous, a soft warm light tinged with the color of tupelo honey emanating from her. Her big brown eyes were clear and concerned and brimming with empathy, her thick brown hair shiny as satin.

"I'm so sorry," I said.

"Sssssh," she whispered, touching her lips with her finger.

"Please forgive me."

"For what?"

"Not saving you."

"You saved me in every way a person can be saved. You know that, soldier."

"I miss you so much."

"I miss you."

The tears in her eyes crested and began to wind down her cheeks, and as she reached up to wipe them, I could see that her burns were gone.

"How could I have wasted so much time?" I said. "Why was I so—"

"We did the best we could. And we did okay."

"Okay? I got you killed. I wasted the little time we had."

"We did okay."

"I'm glad they're going to kill me. I don't want to live without you. I can't."

"Don't say that. You have to fight. Please. I need you to. You can't let them get away with this."

"What's it like where you are? Will we be together again?"

I woke up to see the big man looking down at me.

"Who were you talking to?" he said.

"An angel."

He nodded, as if he understood. "Won't be long now."

"You gots no idea how right you are," Clip said, walking up behind the man and shooting him in the side of his enormous head.

As the now dead man slowly slid off his stool onto the floor, Clip smiled down at me, his brilliant white teeth blinding in contrast to his black skin.

Clipper Jones was a young one-eyed Negro who had been part of the 99th Fighter Squadron, 1st Tactical Unit before suffering the loss of his left eye. He picked up the nickname

Clipper while training at Dale Mabry Field because of the way he would so fearlessly dive down toward the Gulf, fly in low and "clip" the tops of the North Florida pines.

He had helped me on a number of cases and saved my ass on a number of occasions, and though I always paid him and he always took it, I knew everything he did was an attempt to repay me for a debt I never thought he owed.

"Big bastard was psychic. Won't be long now. Sure as shit wasn't, either. Shee-it. The hell they been doin' to you in here?"

"All they could."

"I reckon so. Gotdam, man."

"How'd you find me?"

"I didn't."

"Huh?"

"He didn't. I did," Ruth Ann Johnson said, shuffling into view at the end of my bed, just at the edge of the circle of light.

I was surprised to see her.

A Salvation Army nurse who had served in the war helping wounded soldiers in the South Pacific before getting wounded herself, she and I had never been much more than drinking buddies brought together by our wounds—even though we never really discussed my missing arm or her missing leg. Mine was a source of embarrassment, but hers ... I wasn't sure why she was so reticent to talk about her brave act of sacrifice and heroism.

She had thick blond hair worn above her shoulders and flipped out on the ends, and big blue eyes that looked interested even when they weren't. Small and bright and sweet, Ruth Ann looked like nothing so much as somebody's cute kid sister.

I knew why Clip was here, but why her?

"How'd—"

"I had a nurse friend looking out for you at Johnston's Sanatorium in Tallahassee. She let me know the moment you went missing, and I started playing Jimmy Riley boy detective. It's fun. I see why you do it."

"Did it," I said. "I'm done. Where's Christa?"

"Who?"

"The blonde bitch who likes to play with electricity."

"This fat bastard and his dead twin out there the only bitches here," Clip said. "I could hang 'round and see who show up."

"I need your help getting Jimmy tucked in at my place," Ruth Ann said. "You wanna make with layin' in wait, you can come back later on your own dime."

"Think maybe I will," he said. "Think I just might will."

4

More days spent in a haze of hallucination and humiliation.

Crazed. Confused.

A delirium of drug-induced dreams. Lauren dying over and over again. A Japanese Hitler with a woman's body in a nurses uniform prodding and shocking me over and over again while reading newsreel stories in his best James Cagney. Then Clip walks up behind him and shoots him in the head, but as the gun goes off it's Lauren, and I watch her die, her frail frame crumpling as she collapses onto the floor beside my hospital bed.

After what seemed like years, I finally managed to force my eyes open and keep them that way for a few seconds at a time.

I looked around the dim room.

Small and simple, the modest room was filled with a walnut waterfall-style bedroom set that I could barely make out beneath the pale, narrow beam of the Wabash blackout bulb.

I knew I was at Ruth Ann's because she had been the angel hovering over me with meals, medications, and ministrations in the moments when the fog lifted enough for me to make her out, but until now I hadn't realized I was in her bedroom.

Perfumes and powders, jewelry and makeup lined the mirrored dressing table, the mauve covered stool of which was well worn and faded. A lavender nightgown and matching housecoat hung on the doors of the armoire. I could see myself in the circular mirror on either side of them—an experience as unfortunate as it was unpleasant that confirmed I looked as good as I felt.

Like the footboard of the double bed I was on, the walnut wood of the other furniture I could see was scuffed and scarred.

Ruth Ann's leg was propped in the corner between the dressing table and the armoire.

Far better than the only one I'd ever seen her wear, the prosthetic propped in the corner made the one she regularly used resemble a couple of sticks and an old leather strap. Certain there was a story behind it, I made a mental note to mention it to her sometime. Maybe I'd finally get the real report on who stole the limb in the first place.

The opportunity to ask presented itself almost immediately as the door opened and she sidled in on her crutches.

"Well hiya, soldier," she said, her voice morning fresh and filled with sunshine. "Welcome back. We missed you."

I tried to say something but nothing came out.

She was wearing a blue-and-white-striped cotton playsuit with large white buttons running the length of it and a dress-up bow tied at the waist, a To Hell with Hitler button on her lapel.

"Here," she said, propping herself and her crutches on the side of the bed and retrieving a glass of water from the bedside table. "Wet your whistle."

I did.

"Thanks for all you've done," I said.

Even in my diminished state I knew the food and medication and treatment she had given me had cost her plenty. The only way she could've managed it with all the rationing going on, all the shortages taking place, was to both break the rules and sacrifice her own needs. The thought of either bothered me but good.

And I didn't know which one did worse—her not taking care of herself or stealing meds from wounded servicemen who really needed them.

She shook her head, her blond hair whipping about, and gave me an expression like it was nothing.

"And you shouldn't'a put me in your room."

"Sure, soldier, I should put you on the sofa and let you take your chances."

"Well, I'm better now," I said, "so I'll swap ya."

"Tell you what—I'll arm wrestle you for it."

I laughed. "How long I been out?"

"Let's see. Long enough for the war to end, Hitler to take office, and everyone to learn German."

"Glad I haven't missed much."

We were quiet a moment and I could tell she was trying to work her way into saying something. I knew the dark fabric covering the windows was required for the blackout at night, but I wondered if she kept them on during the day to hide the fact that I was here. And was she a single woman hiding me from nosy neighbors, a guardian angel hiding me from whoever's trying to rub me out, or both?

"Let's have it," I said.

"What?"

"Whatever it is."

"When you're better," she said, "we need to talk."

"It's as bad as all that?"

"Worse."

"Do your best."

"Another time. When you're stronger."

"Now."

"Why so anxious to get your heart hammered on, soldier?"

"You really think you can top Lauren being dead?"

"Oh. I didn't know you knew."

"Well I do. What else you got?"

"You're wanted for murder."

"Oh yeah? Just one?"

"It's serious, soldier."

"I know it is, but doesn't mean it matters to me."

"Harry Lewis is now mayor."

"And I'm the reason," I said.

"You helped Lauren's husband become mayor?"

"It was his consolation prize."

"Yeah?"

"Lauren and I left together. We just didn't arrive at the same place. 'Sides, he really was the best candidate. Howell's bent but bad."

"That's the other thing," she said. "Howell took a powder. They're looking for him same as you, but he vanished."

"What about Walt? Rainer? Ann Everett?"

"No mention of them in the paper."

"You sure?"

"Positive. I've read every word of every issue since you got yourself shot again."

"I've got to speak to Pete," I said. "I gave him all the evidence he needed to put the big squeeze on 'em. Wonder who got to him. Guess he's bent as the rest."

5

C lip and I were in a car he had somehow secured for us, not far from police headquarters watching for my old partner Pete Mitchell.

The car, an English pea-green 1940 LaSalle, obviously belonged to a patriot. A red, white, and blue tag on the front bore a soaring eagle, its talons clutching an American flag shield, and read Buy U.S. Defense Bonds, while a yellow bumper sticker on the back said REMEMBER PEARL HARBOR, Dec. 7, 1941. In the backseat, various war publications with covers—like the one depicting a white American woman being assaulted at the end of bayonets by Jap soldiers in uniform and read JAP BEAST AND HIS PLOT TO RAPE THE WORLD—were mixed in with packets of matches showing falling bombs that read Tokens for Tokyo and buttons that said To HELL with HIROHITO.

I was reclined as best I could be in the passenger seat. Clip was hunched behind the wheel, failing at not looking suspicious.

We were smoking black market cigarettes. "Paper Doll" by the Mills Brothers was on the radio.

"Every cop in town looking for you," he said, "so where our asses go?"

"Bold, huh?"

"I'd say that German bitch done fried your brain but good ... but you did shit like this before she got holt to you."

"Ever find her?"

"No suh, she done gone wit da wind," he said, a big smile on his face. "Bitch be as crazy as you say she be, she might be staking out police headquarters too."

I smiled, and we fell silent a few moments.

The darkish day was wet and cold, but I didn't mind. It was nice just to be out in it—out of the house, out of bed, out of my head for a while.

The papers on the seat between us let me know how much I had missed while I was out of commission—at home and in the war—but nothing was more disturbing than the article about the four young women who had been murdered in the area over the past few weeks.

Eventually, I shifted in the seat and winced, trying not to show just how bad the slightest movement hurt.

"Anything go down," he said, "you be no help at all, will you?"

"I don't know ..." I said. "You could always use me as a body shield."

We sat for hours—something truly challenging for guys as impatient as the two of us.

It seemed as though every cop in town came and went a number of times, but no Pete.

"Maybe he off today," Clip said.

"I'd say so too, but Butch is working."

Butch was Pete's new partner, a hard case and a headcase from Chicago who I'd had more than a few tussles with. He'd actually tried to pin a few murders on me not so long ago and kidnapped Ray, the former Pinkerton and PI I worked for at the time.

"Maybe he and Pete ain't partnered up no more."

"Maybe," I said.

"What now?" he asked.

We drove to Pete's place, a small clapboard house he rented on East Avenue in Millville.

Along the way, we passed house after house with blue star flags in the windows, signifying a family member, most likely a husband or son, was serving in the war. It was astounding how many members of our community were missing from among us, fighting, in part at least, for the homes the flags were displayed in. Other windows in other houses held gold stars, which unlike those the Nazi's made the Jews wear, were a symbol of pride and honor, a recognition that the person serving and the family he left behind had made the ultimate sacrifice.

A car I didn't recognize, a big black Packard, was parked on the side of Pete's in the yard, and I wondered if the confirmed bachelor finally got himself a girl.

It took me a while to walk the short distance from the car to the small front porch. When I finally arrived at the screen door after easing up the stairs, I kicked it a couple of times on the wood frame at the bottom, something I found easier and less painful than lifting my arm to knock.

"Hey fella, how about not kicking my door down," a middle-aged man in gray grime-smeared coveralls said. "Oh," he added, when he saw I was missing an arm, "sorry, soldier. What can I do for you?"

"Who are you?" I asked.

"Who am I? You serious? I'm the guy whose porch you're standing on. Who are you?"

Everything about him said grease. He smelled strongly of it, and it could be seen both on his clothes and under his nails. His dark-complected skin had an unwashed, greasy quality to it, and his slicked-back hair, which was as black as his work boots, was wet with it.

"I'm the guy looking for Pete Mitchell."

"Who?"

"The guy renting this porch and the house it's attached to."

"That's me," he said.

"What's you?"

"I'm not what's his name ... Pete, but I am the poor sap renting this shack."

"Since when?"

"Since the check cleared, pal. What's this about?"

"You know anything about the man that was here before you?"

"Yeah, soldier, I know stuff. He's clean, tidy, and generous."

"What makes you say that?"

"Place was clean and tidy."

"No, the generous part."

"Because," he said, "he left me most of his stuff, mister. Whatta you call it?"

6

F ar more a reflection of her husband and his place in the ruling class of our community, Lauren's grave resembled not at all the woman it was meant to memorialize.

The double marble marker was huge and gaudy with two enormous sculpted hearts tilted toward one another beneath the imposing bold block LEWIS. Lauren Grace was chiseled into the left heart above the cold, cruel dates 1917-1943. Across from hers, in the right heart, Hieronymus Gerald was carved above the single date 1877, and centered beneath them both was Married May 14, 1939.

I had come to mourn, to attempt to connect to Lauren somewhere besides my dreams, but Harry had made it impossible. He had imprisoned her within his pride and possessiveness in death even more than he had in life.

I had left Clip in the car, but there was no need. There was nothing here for me, nothing that required solitude, silence, or privacy.

I wondered if he somehow realized that too when I sensed someone behind me, but as I turned saw Father Keller, a priest at

St. Dominic's, Lauren's priest at the end, standing there, his bright blue eyes moist and sad.

Like Harry, he was old enough to be her dad, his darkish wavy hair beginning to go gray, the dark complexion of his fleshy face rough and wrinkled.

"Wasn't I after thinking I might bump into you here sometime?" he said.

There was only a hint of Irish lilt left in his voice, but it was undeniable.

"I'm terrible sorry we lost her," he added.

"We didn't," I said.

"I just meant we all cared for—"

"I did," I said. "All of it—every bit of it—was my fault."

"It wasn't, but I won't argue with you about it, lad."

I had not liked the man from the moment I met him and thought he was Lauren's lover—the one that came after me. Later, I liked him even less when I discovered he was her confessor, that he knew secrets of hers I was no longer privy to, truths about the transformation she was undergoing, a metamorphosis I was completely unaware of.

"I've been praying for you."

"Well stop," I said, "and fast. Don't need anything from a god who'd do this."

"Thought you said you did it?" he said, his voice gentle, nonconfrontational.

I let that one go.

The cemetery was filled with American flags and commemorative ribbons that fluttered and rippled and snapped in the silence, everything of insubstantial weight being buoyed on the brisk breeze.

"Okay, soldier, have it your way. I'm not trying to sell you anything."

"You're not?"

"No, I'm not."

"Then what?"

"Nothing. Don't want anything. Not trying to ... nothing, but ..."

"Yeah? Let's have it."

"I'd like to help you if I can."

"No thanks."

"I read that you're wanted for murder? Anything in it?"

"If there is, still want to help?"

"Of course," he said, but his voice sounded less sure than his words indicated.

My anger and outrage spiked again, triggered by how little his help for Lauren did her.

"Why didn't you take Lauren to a doctor? Why didn't you get her the help she needed?"

"I'm so sorry. I tried to help her. Thought I was. I sincerely did. And I did encourage her to see a doctor, but I should've insisted. I feel so ... guilty. I'm just ... I know ... I failed her."

"We all did. Me most of all. That's what I'm so sore about."

"I have a letter for you from her in my office."

"What? A what?"

"Told me to give it to you if anything happened to her. It was written a while back. You saw her again after she wrote it. She probably got the chance to tell you everything she wrote, but ..."

I looked away from him, back toward Lauren's grave and beyond. I longed for her so badly I didn't want to live. To have something from her—written to me, for me from her, something her hand penned to me—made me weak, and I could feel my knees beginning to buckle.

Hearing of a letter from her reminded me of the records I had from her counseling sessions with Ann Everett. Were they still in my office? Did I still have an office? I wanted to gather everything I had of Lauren's, anything with a connection to her—every scrap of paper with a scribbled note, every gift, every article of clothing, a stray stocking, an abandoned bra, she had ever left behind, every photograph, every and anything with a scent, a trace, a hint — any and every object that could serve as a conduit to deliver her, however partially, up from the underworld, bring her back, however momentarily, to me.

"This is unrelated, I guess, but Harry came to see me a week or so ago," he said.

I looked at Harry's side of the gravestone again, then back at Keller.

"He really cared about her. Wanted her to be happy. Was glad the two of you had what you had."

He hesitated, but I didn't say anything.

"Said you're the reason he's mayor, that he owes you. Told me if I saw you to tell you to come see him, that he'd help you."

"Let's go get that letter."

"Sure, soldier, but what about the mayor's offer? He's a good person to have on your side."

At what seemed like the exact moment he referred to the new mayor, a chunk of Harry's name shot out from the grave as the round from a high-powered rifle hit the monument.

I dove toward Keller, tackling him, but the second round exploded the back half of his head off and he was dead by the time we hit the ground.

The pain from landing, even partially on the priest, was excruciating, and though I needed to roll, to find cover, it took a moment before I could move.

And then Clip was speeding up in the car, crashing into monuments, knocking over markers, slinging open the door, pulling me in by the scruff of my suit coat, and we were speeding away, rounds ricocheting around us, splintering tree branches, pocking gravestones. And then we were gone.

7

I was propped up on pillows on Ruth Ann's bed, shirt off, trying to appear tough as she sewed me backup.

She was sitting on the edge of the bed, her wooden leg and crutches leaning on the dresser across from her.

"You opened it back up but good, fella," she said. "You keep tearing it apart like this, it never will heal."

"Seemed preferable to letting a rifle round open up my skull."

"That's okay, soldier. I'll keep stitching you back up. I don't mind."

"Actually, it was fine 'til Clip scraped it on the side of the car."

"Shee-it," he said, walking in with a box full of my things, "your ass be dead as that preacher, I hadn't saved it. Again."

"Poor Father Keller," Ruth Ann said without looking up.

"Yeah," I said.

Clip and I had stopped by my room at the Cove Hotel where I had lived for the past couple of years and gotten my things—the few things worth getting anyway—and Clip was now bringing them into the room. We had found my old room at the Cove empty—well, empty of my stuff. The fella renting it now had all his things scattered about nice and homey like. All my worldly possessions were in a couple of boxes in the night manager's office.

I had been the house detective there in trade for my room and had done him more than a few good turns. Not so much for him not to give my room away, apparently, but at least enough that he felt obliged to hold on to my meager belongings and not call the cops when I picked them up—as he had been instructed to do.

I had also wanted to go by my office, but was bleeding too much to make that possible.

The box Clip was struggling with now was full of books and I could tell he was not only unhappy about the weight but the contents.

"Look like readin' all these would make you smart enough not to go and get yourself shot up and kidnapped and tortured and shot at again and have to be taked care of by a nurse and a butler."

I laughed. "A butler?"

"Whatcha call a house nigga that unload boxes and drive a wounded one-armed cracker around?"

"A butler, a chauffeur, and, if the wounded one-armed cracker is me, lucky."

"Well, this here one-eyed whatever is gonna chauffeur his own self home now. Try not to get yourself killed before I get back tomorrow."

"Thanks," I said.

"No need," he said.

"That's sweet," Ruth Ann said.

"Just keep puttin' money in a nigga's pocket," he said. "That all."

"Oh," she said. "Here I was thinking you were—"

She stopped speaking when she saw me withdraw a framed photograph of Lauren from the box next to me on the bed. It was my favorite picture of her—and just seeing it sent me.

Suddenly, the scent of Paris perfume filled my nostrils and I could feel the soft warmth of her skin on my lips and fingertips, taste her wine-tinged tongue.

Lost in Lauren, I was only vaguely aware of Clip silently slipping out of the room.

Ruth Ann remained quiet a long moment, working on my wound with even more concentration. Beneath her blond hair, her blue eyes were narrowed, her mouth parted slightly between her too red lips. She was opposite Lauren in nearly every way— and not just physically.

Lauren's dark eyes were penetrative even in the picture, her intensity and mystery heightened by her thick dark hair and her burn-scarred olive skin.

When I returned the photograph to its box, Ruth Ann's shoulders let down ever so slightly as her tension seemed to be released into the room.

After a few more moments, she said, "So, tell me, what'd you learn today?"

I told her.

"You worried about Pete?"

I nodded.

"What're you gonna do?"

"Find him."

She looked back toward the door Clip had just exited by.

"With Clip's help, right?"

I nodded again.

"Who you think's trying to kill you, fella?"

"Gonna find that out too."

"What's the story with you and Clip? You mind me asking?"

"I don't mind."

"He'd do anything for you," she said. "I can tell. He feels like he owes you, but it seems like more than that. He acts like he's only doing it for the money, but that's just to cover up how much he cares about you."

"Now don't get carried away," I said. "I wouldn't say he's covering up much of anything—especially feelings."

"Well I would."

I nodded as I thought about it.

As I did, something she touched sent currents of pain arcing through me.

"Sorry, soldier, but it's got to be done," she said. "Hold still."

We fell quiet again and I tried not to move.

"I wanna get someone to look at this," she said. "That okay with you?"

"Depends on the someone."

"Give a girl a little trust, would you? I wouldn't cross you up and you know it."

"Okay."

"So?" she said. "What gives? Quit being so cagey. Let's hear it."

"Huh?"

"You and Clip. Spill."

"Not much to it. He got in a jam. I helped him out."

"Come on, soldier. Tell me the story. It'll get your mind off the girl."

Nothing could do that and she knew it—or maybe she didn't. Maybe nobody did. Maybe I was the only one who knew the depth of my depression and obsession. And maybe that was best.

"Tell me the short version," she said. "It won't hurt so bad."

"Clip's got a mouth on him, likes to carry on. Entertains himself with it. Finds it amusing. But sometimes he's the only one who does."

"You two have that in common," she said.

"And he doesn't take anything from anyone. Especially white men in authority."

"Yeah," she said, "y'all got that in common too, but those white men got a name for men like Clip who do it."

"Yes they do. Look up uppity nigger in the dictionary and all it has is a picture of Clip. Anyway, all this means he's been entangled with some of the boys on the force for a few years now. Couple of them always looking for a way to bring him down. And a few years back they found it. I don't know all the details—had something to do with some stolen merchandise—and I don't know if Clip was covering for a friend or if he really was guilty. Didn't matter—not to the two cops taking him down. Whitfield and Dixon. Stolen merchandise was just their invite into his life. They were going in to dismantle it piece by piece—and good too. Don't know for certain if it was true or not, knowing Clip I always suspected it was, but word was Clip had messed around with Dixon's wife."

She finished bandaging me back up and I held it as I read-justed the pillows and reclined a little more.

"And? Come on, soldier. This ain't no Saturday morning serial. Get on with it."

"I could tell by the way they were working the case—not gathering evidence, not following protocol—they knew it wasn't going to trial."

"Whatta you mean?"

"Clip was never leaving custody alive. Hell, he'd never be in custody either. Not really. They were going to go at him hard for a while off campus and then he'd get killed trying to escape."

When I stopped again, she sighed heavily and shook her head.

"And?"

"And I stopped them. Clip feels like he owes me. He does not."

"The hell he doesn't. You saved his life."

"There you go again," I said.

"It's true."

"He saved my life today," I said. "And that's not the first time. Or the fourth."

"So you're saying you two are squared?"

"No. I'm saying I owe him."

She nodded like that explained everything.

"What?"

"That's what I mean," she said. "He's not just trying to repay you. I mean, he is—'cause I don't care what you say, you two are not even, not even close and he knows it—but there's more to it than that. He cares for you."

"Okay. Okay. Enough of that," I said. "So we know why Clip's doing what he's doing. Doesn't explain why you are. Why'd my sometime drinking buddy turn all Nancy Drew and find me, and then all Florence Nightingale and nurse me back to health?"

"Mister, you're a long way from health," she said. "And you sure ain't helping yourself none."

"Sure. Still doesn't answer why. Why're you doing so much for me?"

She shot me an amused look and let out a little-girl giggle. "Same reason as Clip, silly," she said. "Very same reason."

8

That night, Clip was awakened by Pookie, a cousin who stayed with him sometimes, with the news that a cop was at the front door asking to see him.

"Asking or demanding?" Clip asked.

"I 'on't know. Why?"

"Need to know if trouble's waiting for me out there."

"Clip, po-leese always be trouble."

"Good point," Clip said, removing the revolver from the table beside his bed and shoving it in the back of his suspendered pants.

Clip's shack in Shine Town was tiny, and it didn't take him long to get to the front door.

Located in the easternmost section of St. Andrews originally known as East End, Shine Town was the Negro community named after a big moonshiner named Shine who moved in after the mill closed, and made and sold rum. Before him, back when it was East End, a man named Thompson ran a saw mill. Lumber from the head of East Bay was floated down to the head of Massalina Bayou, and the mill workers lived in homes built by the mill owner, known as the quarters.

Clip stepped outside to see a thick-bodied middle-aged white man in a day-wrinkled shirt. Weary and in serious need of a shave, the cop didn't appear to pose much of a threat.

Didn't mean he didn't.

"You Clipper Jones?"

"I is, but I didn't know she was white."

"Huh?"

"Nothin'. What you want?"

"Got a message for Jimmy Riley."

"Then send him a telegram."

"It's important. His old partner Pete is missing and I need to talk to him. I need his help."

"Who's help? What was that name again?"

"Look, it's on the level. I swear it. I want to talk to Jimmy. I'm gonna ask for his help, not arrest him. I know he hasn't killed anybody."

The look Clip gave him made him amend his statement.

"I mean I know he's not guilty of murder."

Clip smiled.

"Will you take me to him?"

"What's your name?"

"Rogers. Delton Rogers. Used to work with Jimmy back when he and Pete were partners. I'm a friend."

"I know all his friends and none of 'em is cops. Same as the rest of us."

"Tell you what. You give Jimmy the message. No harm in that. He'll want to hear what I have to say. Just let him decide. Give him the message."

"See," Clip said. "Tol' you all you needed was a telegram."

Later that night, I convinced Ruth Ann to drive me in her '41 Ford Club Coupe to my old office at the Parker Detective Agency.

We were smoking Chesterfields and the car was filled with smoke.

The November night was cold, and in addition to her woolen

Reefer coat, Ruth Ann wore a plaid head kerchief with a self-fringe, just a bit of her blond hair visible just above her forehead.

Downtown was a dichotomy. Since the war began, many of the places on the main drag were open all night, but just one block away in any direction it was deserted—empty streets bathed in pale moonlight, dew-dampened surfaces shimmering silently, parking lots, businesses, alleyways barren, appearing suddenly and abruptly abandoned.

Our offices were in a walkup on Harrison just down from the Tennessee House and Ritz Theater, where Hitchcock's Shadow of a Doubt was playing at the moment, and it was as haunted for me as any other place on the planet. Haunted in the way the little house in the Cove where I had my arm blown off was.

Headlights on dim, the top halves painted black, we crept around a while, searching for signs of cops and the perfect place to park, as Tommy Dorsey sang "In the Blue of the Evening."

Deciding breaking into the old building from the back was best, we eased down Grace, beams followed closely by car body piercing the low flung fog.

Ray Parker, the guy whose agency it had been, was a big, squarish former Pinkerton who had been like a father to me—right up until I had killed him.

Creeping up the back stairs while Ruth Ann waited in the car, I trailed the bobbing little beam down the hallway to July's desk.

July.

Our Rosie-the-riveter receptionist had worn her hair in a short feather-cut, pin curls around her ears and on top of her head, and had been as cute as someone's yappy little puppy. She had worked hard, worshipped Ray, and wanted nothing more than to be Nancy Drew.

Her desk looked untouched, the strewn papers in the same place as the night I had searched through them to find her murderer.

I pictured her there, two-finger typing, answering the phone with attitude, filling in logs, sorting through ration tickets. Though not too many years younger than me, she had seemed like such a kid, had been such a kid.

The hours we had spent together in this dingy little place.

She and Ray both dead.

It was hard to believe what once had been an impressive agency was down to a wounded, one-armed, lovesick sap wanted by the police.

I stood at the door to my office, taking it in, the small circle of light falling on stacks of books, a dusty old chess set, an uncluttered desk and uncomfortable chair, a few unhung paintings on the floor, a General Electric shelf-charging portable radio, a Motorola Spinet with records stacked around it, and around and among it all, the fingerprint powder and evidence markers and police-trampled appearance that even in the dark whispered it was a crime scene.

When I looked at my chair, pushed back from my desk and at an odd angle, an old empty wooden chair was all I saw, but as I looked at anything else in the room, in my periphery I would see July's lifeless, crumpled body slumped in it.

Ghosts.

July's death haunted me but good, but it was Lauren's presence here that most affected me. It was here, in this small room she had first walked into my life, the scent of Paris perfume wafting up from the wake behind her.

She had disarmed me with her disconcerting honesty, unconventional beauty, and her complete lack of pretense and illusion.

My desire for her had been instant and incomprehensible.

Beneath her dark brown hair, combed smooth across the top and hanging in soft curls above her shoulders, worn lower on the right side of her face to conceal the burns, her otherwise flawless skin seemed nearly too perfect, the almond eyes beneath the razor-sharp eyebrows nearly too dark, too deep, too ... Nearly, but not too.

"Of the infidelity cases you investigate, how many of the people turn out to be cheating?" she had asked.

"Nearly all."

"Really?"

"Most people don't come to us the first time they have suspicions."

"So what percentage?"

I shrugged.

Her silhouette-style black dress emphasized her trim waist and narrow hips and grew broad above her breasts. The war had made stockings mostly a thing of the past, but her dress showed plenty of pale leg beneath black silk stockings, the backs of which had seams running down them. The rest of the girls had to go bare-legged and draw seams down the back of their legs with black eyeliner to give the illusion of stockings, but not Mrs. Harry Lewis. Her justification for this pass from this small wartime sacrifice was that they helped conceal the burn scars on her legs.

Her two-tone, thick high heels brought together the black of her dress, its white collar and highlights, and the white of her gauntlet gloves and clutch bag.

"How many? I want to know."

"It's hard to say."

"How long have you been doing this?"

"A few years," I said.

Gracefully, she crossed her long, shapely legs and straightened out her skirt. Her movements were as smooth and elegant as the silk stockings gripping her gams. They were dark, but you could still make out the burns down her right leg if you knew where to look.

"So, of the cases you've worked, how many were guilty of cheating?"

"All of them," I said.

Her eyes widened. She then exhaled heavily and fell back

into her chair, the expression on her face a curious one, as if I had just shared a strange good news.

"So the fact that I'm here almost guarantees my husband is cheating."

"Do you love your husband?"

"Very much."

"If he is cheating, are you going to leave him?"

She shook her head.

"Then don't do this."

"I've got to," she said.

"Why? Why do you want to know?"

"I love my husband, Mr. Riley."

"So don't—"

"Like a father," she said. "I'm not in love with him—not like a wife. I care about him a great deal. I owe him ... well, everything. But if I knew he had someone ..."

She had trailed off, but seemed to need to say more, so I waited.

"It would be a great comfort to me."

Standing in the darkened doorway now, her words not only echoed through the room, but through me.

And her words were what I was here for.

Easing inside, I stepped carefully, as if avoiding apparitions, making my way over to the phonograph and removing the recordings Ann Everett had secretly made of Lauren's counseling sessions, forced to pocket my light in order to carry them.

Records clutched to my chest with my left hand, I stumbled out into the hallway, along the corridor, and back down the stairs.

Reaching the door, I realized I was going to have a problem opening it when the only arm I had was holding the records, but then a guy with a gun stepped out of the dark alcove and suddenly I had more pressing problems to worry about.

9

"Hiya, solider," he said, pressing the pistol into the small of my back. "Whatta you say we take a rittle stroll?"

"Sure," I said. "I could use some air."

"Then ret's take in some air."

There seemed to be something faintly foreign, even exotic in his accent, but he was speaking so softly I couldn't be sure, every syllable snaking out of his mouth in whispered hisses.

We stepped out of the building, off the concrete pad, and into the parking lot, and I heard him gently close the door behind us.

A few random desultory sounds came across the buildings from some of the all-night activities on Harrison, but back here it was desolate and dark, our footfalls and the soft whistle of the wind the only noises.

"We headed anywhere in particular?" I asked. "Or just strolling?"

"Hang a reft."

I did, all the while hoping Ruth Ann wouldn't see us and try to intervene.

Glancing over to the right side of the lot where she was

parked, I could see she was asleep behind the wheel, her head tilted back on the seat at an angle.

At the far edge of the opposite side of the parking lot in a dark corner beneath an oak tree, a Studebaker sat idling, its evanescent exhaust coiling up a few feet before vanishing into the damp night air.

As we neared it, I could see that the vehicle was in pristine condition, appearing nearly new though it had been almost a year since the company had abandoned regular passenger car production. The final civilian car had rolled off the assembly line in January of '42. The fact that it had painted trim meant it was a special Blackout edition and was among the last to be produced.

"Who's in the car?" I asked.

"Man with a job for you."

"That he's gonna offer to me at gunpoint?"

"He's really hoping you'a take it."

"I'm seriously considering it," I said. "I really am."

He laughed.

The car was a six-passenger Presidential Deluxe-style Land Cruiser with a black roof, whitewall tires, which were extremely rare right now, and a back glass with ventilating wings.

When we reached it, the man behind me stepped around and opened the back door.

I took a step back.

He was a short, thin kid who looked to be in his late teens. He had no hat on and his thick bowl-cut black hair looked like a melted record atop his head.

He was Japanese.

"Didn't get enough of us at Pearl Harbor?" I said. "Taking us out one by one now?"

He waved me into the car with the small gun and I climbed inside. When he closed the door, any ambient light from the street vanished and I was alone in the dark with what looked to be an older version of the kid who was now leaning on the car looking in at us.

"I ... ah ... had ah nothing to do with the attack," he said. "I am American citizen just rike you."

I didn't respond.

"Ah ... you ... have ah ... no doubt heard about the murders."

He kept his gaze straight ahead and spoke very softly.

"I've been a little out of circulation," I said, "but I've heard a thing or two ... read a few more in the paper. For all I know some of them may even be true."

"Young women," he said.

He didn't say anything else right away, but I waited, knowing there was more to come.

"Butchered."

The kid leaning against the car shook out a smoke and lit it, his little revolver dangling from his finger as he did.

"Beautiful girls ah hacked into ah pieces."

The report in the paper indicated that the murders had been particularly brutal, but there was no mention of anything like that. Was he exaggerating or did he know more than was being printed?

"The investigation ah being conducted by the ah porice is yielding nothing," he said. "Which mean they ah either ah incompetent or ah corrupt."

"A little over a year ago I was one of them," I said, "and I can tell you they're neither."

He reached up and turned on a light, and when my eyes had adjusted I could see that he was a thick middle-aged Japanese man with thick black hair and thick orangish skin. He was togged to the bricks in a three-button tan Glen Plaid sports coat and solid medium brown wool slacks with pleats and cuffs, a hand-painted tie in a thick Windsor knot, and brown and tan wingtips.

"Whato other ah expranation is there?"

"They haven't caught a break in the case yet. They will. What's your interest? Why're you telling me all this?"

"Niece. Missing. Sister daughter. You find outo if she ah one of his ah victims. If not, you find her."

If he was making any effort to melt into Uncle Sam's big pot, I couldn't tell it, the way he spoke only adding to the alien nature of his presence here.

"There' no agency anymore," I said. "I'm in no condition to work a case even if there was."

"I know what ah happen. What you did. What condition you ah in."

"I'm wanted by the police for a little murder of my own."

"That make you ah more quarified, not ress. Same as us. We cannot go to porice. If we did they ah send us back to ah Manzanar. Even if we could, they no care for ah Jap girl."

"I could be the most qualified person on the planet," I said. "I'm not doing it. I can't."

"I'm ah noto asahking."

On cue, the kid tapped the glass with the barrel of the gun, smoke curling up from his cigarette, backlit by a streetlamp as he did.

"So," I said, "I ah taka the case or you ah kill me?"

"No. Starto with sreeping girl in ah car. Then brother. Mother. Father. Nigger friend. Then ah you."

I didn't respond.

"You go talk to niece mother. Sister. You say I ah sent."

"I don't even know who you are."

"Tell her brother send. Car ah pick you up ah here tomorrow ah night. You be here or ah girl get it."

"Then ah," I said, "I'll ah be here."

10

The next morning I awoke in Ruth Ann's bed to the smell of coffee and eggs and bacon. She was standing in the doorway holding a tray of breakfast, a paper on one side, a vase of fresh-cut flowers on the back corner of the other.

There was something different about her and it took me a minute to catch up to what it was. She had dyed her hair and was now a brunette. It was fixed differently too—sort of down on one side.

In fact, it seemed that everything about her was different.

"Morning, soldier," she said. "How ya feelin'?"

I gave her a groan and tried to sit up.

My shirt was off, my piece of right arm exposed—sending my already heightened self-consciousness into the hyperactivity of a hophead.

It took a while, but I finally managed a sort of semi-upright position, the pain in my abdomen making me nauseous and lightheaded. Quickly and awkwardly, I yanked the thin sheet and bedspread up, using my still uncomfortable left hand to cover my right shoulder and stump.

"Hope you're hungry. You're gonna need your strength, you keep doing all you're doing, fella."

I gave her a half-hearted smile and thanked her.

"Eat this and I'll give you something for that pain," she said, nodding toward my midsection as she placed the tray in my lap. Touching my stubbled face tenderly, she added, "I worry about you, soldier. I really do. You trying to kill yourself?"

"Not actively, no."

"Trying or not ... you're doing a pretty damn good job of it."

"Sorry, Mom."

"Eat up. I'll be back in a minute with something that'll make you want to marry me."

When she left, I forced myself to eat a little though I had no appetite. The bacon was thick and crispy and the coffee was hot and strong, and I wondered again at how she was able to get such good food and medicine for me with all the rations and shortages.

As I ate, I looked around the room. At some point while I was sleeping she had straightened up, unpacking and organizing my things, placing the picture of Lauren on the table beside the bed, stacking the recordings of her sessions next to a phonograph in what had been an empty corner the night before.

And then I noticed the other thing that was different about Ruth Ann. She had swapped out prosthetic legs. Now the wooden crutch-like leg was propped between the dressing table and armoire and she was wearing the good one.

When she returned to the room, I noticed how much more smoothly and quickly she was able to walk now.

"Take this and eat a little more," she said, handing me a large white pill.

I did.

"I got that information you wanted."

I had no idea what she was talking about and it must have shown on my face.

"About those girls," she said. "The victims."

I only vaguely remembered mentioning them to her, and I certainly didn't ask her to get information about them for me.

"My friend who works in the morgue says he's never seen anything like it. The bodies are bisected and there's no blood. But how they're keeping something so bizarre out of the paper is the real mystery."

"Bisected?"

"Cut in half at the waist. Completely in two. Can you imagine?"

"I can," I said, dropping my fork onto the plate and tossing my napkin over it.

"Sorry."

"Don't be. Keep on."

"All the girls are young and look alike. Dark hair. Dark eyes. He said the things done to the bodies and the way they're displayed is the strangest thing you've ever seen."

"Like what?"

"Like they should be in a museum or gallery or something ... like the guy is making some sort of deranged art exhibit."

11

C lip and I met Delton Rogers near the National Guard Armory on Sixth Street between Jenks and Grace.

Built a few years before the war, it had served as a temporary headquarters for Tyndall Field, but was now home to the Rationing Board.

We were across the street, watching both the traffic passing by on Sixth and the people going in and out of the armory. As usual during the war years, downtown was congested, big gray buses adding to the mix of cars, cabs, trucks, and trailers.

"Jimmy," Delton said as he walked up.

"Delt."

"How ya been?"

"Been better," I said. "Not gonna lie. You?"

"Sorry as hell to hear about—well, everything."

"Thanks."

"You look like you're in a hell of a lot of pain."

We were standing next to a Packard parked on the corner of Jenks, the smoke curling up from our hands and out of our mouths quickly swept up and carried away into the hazy day by the brisk breeze. The Packard was a green convertible with the top down, the interior of which appeared to have been rained in a time or two.

Clip, who thought Delton might be setting me up and half expected an ambush at any moment, continually scanned the area, pacing around to see from all sides.

"He always this jumpy?" Delt asked.

"Cops make him nervous," I said. "What can I do for you, Delt?"

"Well, first I guess I wanted to shake the hand of the man who killed a legend."

Ray had earned his status as legend—early in his career as a Chicago cop, then as a Pinkerton, and finally as a private detective with his own agency. Everyone respected him. Most people feared him. Even the cops.

He extended his hand—his right one at first, then realized his mistake and switched to his left. I didn't shake it.

"Come on, fella. Don't be sore. We're all impressed as hell. How'd you do it? Was it in the back?"

"I oughta shoot your dumb ass in the back right now," Clip said.

"Sorry, soldier," he said, ignoring Clip as if he didn't exist. "It's just ... you got one arm. And it ain't even the one attached to your shooting hand. How the hell did you kill Ray Parker?"

"Where's Pete?" I asked. "What's going on?"

"He's missing. I have no idea. Was hoping you knew something."

"Me?"

"He was working them murders you was involved with, then he just vanished. Poof. Gone."

"You saying he didn't make any arrests in the case?"

"No. Why?"

"I gave him the goods on Howell, Rainer, Cliff Walton, and Ann Everett right before I left town. He was going to bring them in.

That's the last time I spoke to him—and that was on the phone."

"He never brought anybody in. Least not as I know of. Certainly never made any arrests."

"So I'm still a suspect for the murders in that case. I thought I was just wanted for what happened with Ray."

"What did happen with Ray?"

"If Howell wasn't arrested, how is Harry Lewis mayor already?"

"He won the election. Howell dropped out. Left town I think. No scandal or anything. Put out a statement about his health being bad or something. Mr. Lewis took office as soon as he was elected."

I shook my head.

"You sayin' you didn't kill any of those people—not even Ray?"

"I'm saying I didn't kill any of those people except for Ray."

We were quiet a moment as he seemed to ponder what I'd said.

"Why're you reaching out to me, Delt? Telling me all this?"

"I'm worried about Pete. Thought you might help me find him."

"What about you boys taking care of your own?"

"Far as I'm concerned, you're one of us," he said. "And things ain't right at the station. Lots of new faces. Don't know who to trust. And no one seems to be trying all that hard to find Pete. It's like those girls they found is the only case that matters."

"What can you tell me about them?"

"Just that we got some honest-to-god sex killer here in our little town. The things he does to them ... We all want to catch him. But nothing's happening on that one either. Nothing seems to be happening on anything."

"You saying somebody's stopping anything from happening?"

"No. Hell no. I'd get strung up I said anything like that, Jimmy, and you know it."

After leaving Rogers, Clip and I drove down Jenks to Eleventh Street and over to Payton Rainer's sanatorium.

The last time I had seen Rainer he had been pointing a gun at me.

Involved in a plot to blackmail Lauren into getting Harry to drop out of the Panama City mayoral race, Rainer should've been arrested along with Frank Howell, the mayor at the time, Cliff Walton, Harry's head of security who was really working for Howell, and Ann Everett, a counselor Lauren and I had seen. Instead, they were free and Pete was missing.

The sanatorium was in an old converted hotel surrounded by an enormous cement wall with steel gates locked and chained.

And from all appearances it had been abandoned.

The quack had flown the coop. But where had he gone?

He and the others had helped kill Lauren. I would not stop until I gave them some help of my own.

12

"You know we goin' to hell for this," Clip said.

We were at St. Dominic's on Harrison breaking into Father Keller's office to retrieve the letter from Lauren he mentioned before getting gunned down next to her grave.

"All the shit we've done," I said, "and you think this is what's gonna do it?"

"This damn sure tip the scales."

"Seriously? Think about all we've done."

"You right. We's already headed there. This just seal the deal fo sho."

"Lauren told me there was no such thing as hell," I said.

"The hell you say. No such thing as hell. Shee-it."

"Said it was just projections of fear and hate, judgmentalism and condemnation, that the only hells are the ones of our making —well, those and being separated from our beloved."

Suddenly my eyes were stinging and I had to blink several times.

"Beloved? What the hell, fella?"

"Sorry. Love in general. God and all that. And our lovers in particular."

"Don't know about all that shit," he said. "Still say we goin' to hell for this."

As we passed through the sanctuary, I remembered seeing Lauren here when I was following her, recalled how kind the priest had been to her, and I was aggrieved again for what had happened to him. I don't think what I did could be called prayer, but I hesitated a moment, thinking of him, grateful, wishing him well.

When we reached his office, we discovered that like the front door of the church, it wasn't locked.

"Can't exactly break in when everything's unlocked," I said.

"We may not be breakin', but we damn sure enterin'."

The small office was filled with books and piles of papers. A coatrack in the corner held a cheap black suit, a couple of clerical shirts, an umbrella, and well-worn cassock.

"God almighty," Clip said. "We gotta find one piece of paper in this haystack?"

He moved to begin the search, but I grabbed him by the arm to stop him.

"Give me a minute," I said.

I stood there taking it all in. Each stack. Every pile. Letting my vision float around, alighting quickly and gently on each surface.

And then I saw it.

On the right-hand corner of his small wooden desk, beneath a black leather Bible, the edges of an envelope could be seen peeking out of the pages of a bound black notebook.

I walked over, removed the Bible, opened the notebook to confirm, then took the Bible and the notebook, and left the room.

"That Sherlock Holmes shit impressive as hell," Clip said.

"Wasn't what that was."

"You really stealin' a priest's Bible? Shee-it. I only thought we's going to hell before. Now I know it."

My Dearest Jimmy,

I have so much to say to you and such a short time to say it. If you're reading this, then chances are I died. Those chances are looking more and more likely these days, and I don't want that to happen without me getting to tell you just how much I love you.

I was back at Lauren's grave, sitting on a small cement bench beneath the shade of an oak tree, reading the letter she had written me days before her death.

Because I had found her, because she had spent her final few hours with me, I was sure she had told me everything in person that she had written here, but it didn't matter. I would read and reread this love letter from her every day until I joined her in the big beyond, often tracing the curve of her letters with the tip of my finger—the pages providing a tactile as well as spiritual connection.

It was dangerous to be here—and not just because whoever was trying to kill me had already tried here before, but because I might be spotted and the cops alerted—but I didn't want to be anywhere else.

Traces of Father Keller's blood still stained the sandy dirt, faint splatters of it spread across Lauren's marble slab.

I couldn't see Clip but I knew he was around, keeping watch with his one good eye, which was plenty good enough.

I know you don't understand right now, but I do love you more deeply, more profoundly than you can imagine. I've never loved anyone like this, never been loved by anyone the way you have loved me. Even now, I know you love me. I hear it in every cruel, sarcastic remark, see it in your anger and frustration, have felt it in all the ways you've tried to help me lately without even knowing what's been going on.

Meeting you has saved me. Being with you has caused me to wake up. Our love, mine for you and yours for me, has forever changed me. And though it is us, from us, a part of us, it also is beyond us. Through you I've experienced a love that I can only describe as divine.

This experience has been overwhelming for me, and I know I

have not handled it right. I'm so very sorry for that. I know you've not understood and that you've felt betrayed, rejected, abandoned. I can see why you would feel that way, but in my heart, in my actions, I have never done anything but love and care for you. I just wish now that I had done those things better.

Please—

13

I stopped reading and looked up as I sensed someone approaching.

It was Harry Lewis, Lauren's wealthy, much older husband, now a widower and the new mayor of Panama City.

"I wondered how long it'd be before I ran into you here," he said, sitting down on the bench next to me.

Quickly folding up the letter, I looked around us as I placed it in my coat pocket.

"It's just me," he said. "I'm alone."

I didn't say anything, just thought about how lonely Lauren's absence left us both.

"Guess I've never been more alone," he said. "It was hard as hell when my first wife died, but I got through it—largely with Lauren's help. She thought I saved her, but it was really she who saved me. Now, not only do I not have her, but my new job is far more isolating than I ever could have guessed. I'm sure you've heard about those poor girls that have been found."

Clip appeared behind us, gun drawn but down at his side.

Harry turned to look at him, holding his hands up.

I nodded at Clip. "Everything's jake. Harry's okay. We're just gonna have ourselves a nice little chat."

Clip holstered his weapon and backed away, but I knew he wouldn't go far. Eventually, Harry lowered his hands and turned back toward me.

"How is it that you're already mayor?" I asked. "And that Howell's not in jail?"

"I have no idea. I believed what you told me the night you called, but there were no arrests and then Howell dropped out of the race and off the map. I thought you said you had proof. I thought arrests were imminent."

"I did. They were. But I wake up from a coma to find that the detective I gave everything to, my old partner Pete Mitchell, is missing, and that all those involved have taken the big fade."

"You're certain you were right about everything?"

"No question."

"The fact that Walt disappeared too gives great credence to what you told me."

Cliff Walton had been employed by Harry, but had really been working for Howell, his opposition, double crossing Harry, controlling and blackmailing Lauren.

"You haven't heard from him again?" I asked.

"Not a word."

"So they're all gone?"

"Meaning the people who took her from us are out there somewhere living their lives like she'll never be able to again. We can't have that. No sir."

Did he know I was one of them, that I was as responsible as anyone for Lauren's death? More than anyone.

"Tell me that's not acceptable to you," he added.

It wasn't. I had already lived longer than I thought I would. But now I find there are things to square, justice to serve. Now I plan to make sure we all get what we deserve. Couldn't very well meet it out for them and not myself.

"It is not," I said, so stunned by him saying she was taken from us I was unable to say more.

We fell silent a moment, and the serenity of the cemetery came out of the background and into the foreground and I felt a peace that I had heretofore only experienced in Lauren's presence. Was she here with us? Did she find it amusing to see me and Harry sitting together next to her grave?

"I know what you meant to her," he said.

I nodded and waited, but he didn't say anything else. Did he know just how much? Could he? Could anyone?

I said, "I know what you did for her."

Shortly before his death, Coolidge Brown—Lauren's father, Harry's best friend, and the vice president of Harry's bank—had used his position of trust to provide reckless and unsecured loans for friends and embezzle a small fortune for himself. When Harry discovered what he was doing, he confronted him, demanding his resignation and threatening to squawk.

Secretly consumed with envy, Coolidge invited Harry over to his home ostensibly to apologize and discuss restitution, but really to take Harry down with him and his family. At gunpoint, Coolidge set his house on fire, dousing his wife, his kids, and his boss with kerosene. Not only had Harry acted bravely and saved Lauren's life, but he also covered her dad's crimes with his own money, burying the scandal with him. He provided for Lauren through high school and even some college, eventually asking her to take the place of his deceased wife.

Harry had always been good to Lauren. I think the only truly selfish thing he ever did was to ask her to be his wife—something she didn't feel she could say no to.

"We both loved her," he said.

"We did," I said.

"I owe you," he said. "And not just because I wouldn't be mayor if it weren't for you, but for all you did for Lauren, all you meant to her. I will see what I can do about the trouble you're in with the police. In the meantime, use my resources to find those responsible for killing my wife and your ... And let me know what I can do to help. I assure you, I cannot abide them not paying for what they've done. No sir. Cannot. And surely finding them will help your case as well."

14

I was blindfolded in the backseat of a Buick bouncing down a highway in the dark, the guy next to me jamming the gun into my side reeking of the briny smell of the sea and fish and the oaky odor of a wood fire.

It was the middle of a moon-bright night, and I was exhausted and in pain, raw from reading Lauren's letter, spent in every single way.

When I had showed up at the appointed time to the parking lot behind our old office, the two Japanese men waiting for me withdrew their weapons and insisted that I wear a blindfold for the protection of Bunko Matsumoto—the woman whose daughter was missing—and the group hiding from the authorities she was a part of.

I had no idea where we were, but based on the sounds and the speed of our unimpeded progress, I could tell we were out of town on one of North Florida's desolate lost highways.

When we eventually arrived and I was led out of the car, I could hear the surf and feel the Gulf breeze, and I knew we were somewhere along the coast.

I walked slowly, hesitantly, fearful of falling, finding it difficult to get traction in the sand. The guy behind me shoved me often and I stumbled forward, nearly but never quite tripping and falling.

As the blindfold was removed and my eyes adjusted, I could see we were standing inside the natural barrier formed by a group of sand dunes, the sea oats atop them waving in the wind.

The full moon shimmered across the surface of the black sea and cast shadows on the sand.

At first it was just me and the two Japanese men who brought me here, as we waited for Bunko Matsumoto's arrival.

For a while neither of them said anything, the incoming tide and billowing breeze the only sounds swirling around us, but then one turned suddenly toward the Gulf.

"Look ... there ..." he said, pointing out past the beach toward the water slightly down from us. "There's another one."

The second man, the one with the gun, turned to look, and I followed the gazes of both men.

It took a few moments, but eventually I saw it too.

There, bathed in moonlight, like a black monster cresting the dark waters of the Gulf, a German submarine could just barely be seen.

It was interesting the visceral response seeing the U-boat had on me. Instantly, I felt exposed, vulnerable, and was overwhelmed with the feeling that I needed to report it, to find one of the lookout towers that had been erected every twelve miles along the coastline and make sure they too had spotted it.

By contrast, the two men with me were nonchalant, finding the sighting only mildly interesting.

Of course I knew the German sea wolves were trolling American shipping lanes—and finding what they were looking for, taking out vessels at a rate of two per day—and I had heard many fishermen claim to have seen them in our area, not far from shore. But to see one this close to land, to my hometown was a surreal experience.

Eventually, Bunko Matsumoto arrived and the sub submerged and wartime life went on.

"I'm sorry for the way you have been treated," she said with only the slightest hint of an accent, "but we can't take any chances. Your government is at war against us."

"Y'all started it."

"Not Japan. American citizens. I'm an American citizen. So are all those imprisoned in the internment camps. You saw the German sub out there a few minutes ago? You have far more to fear from it than all the Japanese-Americans combined. Where are the German relocation camps?"

I had nothing for that so I let it go.

From her sharp monotone voice and appearance, and the rigidity of her pinched expression, it was obvious that Bunko Matsumoto was not a woman to be messed with. Her no-nonsense glasses and haircut and clothes were all utilitarian and unattractive. There was no question she was imposing and strong-willed, but there was also something overly earnest and humorless about her, and I wondered was it a result of the circumstances under which we were meeting or her natural state.

"We blindfolded you so you wouldn't see the way to our hide-out, but at the last minute we decided to bring you here to the beach. We are all wanted by the police, by the government. For what? For being of Japanese descent. That is our only crime."

She carefully withdrew a worn and wrinkled Western Union telegram from the inside of her coat pocket. She started to hand it to me then remembered my one arm was tied down to my waist.

She then said something in Japanese and the guy behind me removed the rope holding my arm down.

"Do you know where I was when I receive this telegram from our government that my husband had been killed fighting with the United States Army for his country? I was in prison. My country, the one my husband died for, had taken everything from us except what I could carry in two small suitcases, had me locked up like a common criminal in Manzanar, an internment camp, as if I were some sort of a prisoner of war."

After hearing the Japanese man from the night before reference Manzanar, I had researched it a bit and found that it was a relocation camp for citizens of Japanese descent. Situated on the edge of the desert along the eastern slope of the Sierra Nevada, Manzanar, California, was a beautiful, harsh, haunting place where something horrible was happening.

"We got the so-called Civilian Exclusion Order," she continued, "telling us we were going to have to move out of our homes. And our lives were changed forever. You are missing an arm and I know the story behind it. I also know about your great love and loss, Lauren, so perhaps you know a bit of how random, arbitrary, and capricious life can be, Mr. Riley. But you've never experienced true powerlessness. You've never been as helpless and hopeless as having your own country turn on you and tell you your life as you have known it was over."

"No," I said. "I haven't."

Lightning flashed in the distance out over the Gulf and there was a slight but perceptible shift in the atmosphere.

"We became numbers. No longer names. No longer people. We were given one week to liquidate all our possessions. One week. I didn't have much, but what I did I lost. Lost forever, do you get that? I was forced to leave it behind as spoils for those who happen to be of different descent."

When the lighting flashed again, I scanned the undulating waters for signs of the sub, but was unable to see anything in the brilliant but brief illumination.

"You cannot imagine the fear and frustration, the confusion and acute uncertainty. What could we do? We could get next to nothing for the things we had worked so hard for or we could get nothing. I know a man who sold a thirty-room hotel for three-hundred dollars. His brother sold his new 1941 Ford truck for twenty-five. Family heirlooms from generations and generations ago for a fraction of what they would be worth if they had no sentimental value. But, of course, as familial treasures they were priceless."

As the lightning flashed again, it was obvious a storm was moving rapidly toward us.

"When we saw our chance a small group of us escaped. We've come across the continent to hide in huts like savages. I lost my home, my freedom, my heritage, my life, and then my husband. I cannot take losing my Miki too."

From another coat pocket she withdrew a picture and handed it to me.

The photograph was of a beautiful young woman with enormous, dark almond-shaped eyes and long, thick, shiny black hair.

"Find her for me, Mr. Riley."

"Why me? Surely there's someone else you can—"

"There is no one else. I told you, we've checked you out thoroughly. I know you, the sort of man you are. I know what you have done for love. I also know you cannot go to the authorities, can't turn us in."

And there was the real reason.

The outer bands of the storm reached us and it began to rain —not hard or heavy, but constant and cold.

If Bunko Matsumoto felt it at all, she gave no indication, and I wondered if she could feel anything at all anymore.

I slipped the picture in my coat pocket and we stood there in silence in the rain for a long moment, no one moving, no one saying anything.

"I'm waiting for an answer, Mr. Riley," she said eventually. "Do I have your word?"

I opened my mouth to give it to her, but before anything came out an enormous explosion rocked us all back and lit up the night sky with what looked like red and orange lightning made of liquid fire striking the earth beneath the silent, seemingly indifferent moon.

15

I t looked like the Gulf was on fire.

Red and orange flames in the rain.

Black smoke billowing up toward the milk-pale moon.

A cargo ship ablaze, floating in a sea of fire.

What I didn't know then, what I found out later, was that the four-hundred-foot cargo ship was filled with ten thousand tons of fuel oil. Too heavy to anchor in St. Andrew Bay, the weight of the ship also forced it to venture beyond the ten-fathom curve considered safe from the unseen U-boats under the surface of the Gulf waters.

Because German U-boats had put some five hundred million tons of Allied shipping on the bottom of the ocean floor, leading to a critical shortage of cargo ships needed to keep the Allied war effort going, the U.S. Maritime Commission chose sixteen sites, including Brunswick, Georgia, where this one was built, to quickly construct the Liberty ships.

Using sixteen thousand workers, the JA Jones Construction Company quickly and steadily built Liberty ships that were 441 1/2 feet long and 57 feet wide, with a draft of nearly 28 feet, and capable of hauling ten thousand tons across vast ocean distances.

Having had two full decks running the length of the vessel and seven watertight bulkheads rising to the upper deck, the Liberty allowed for five cargo holds located forward and aft of the central engine room. In these immense holds, it carried weapons, ammunition, food, tools, hardware, vehicles, even at times troops—anything and everything that might be needed for the war effort all around the world. This particular one had been fitted to carry fuel. Two one-and-a-half-ton torpedoes struck the port side—one about midship, the other near the stern—and suddenly most of the thirty-five sailors awoke in hell.

"Do you have a boat?" I yelled.

No one answered.

"Do you have a boat?" I said again.

I looked around, scanning the area. In the distance, I could see a small marina and a forty-foot cruiser.

"Whose is that?" I asked. "The cruiser. Whose is it?"

"Not ours," Bunko said.

"We're gonna borrow it," I said. "Come on. Let's go."

Neither man moved.

"We've got to get out there as soon as possible," I said. "Let's go. Now."

The two men looked at Bunko. She nodded.

"You turn them in and I'll have you killed," she said to me.

"Find a phone," I yelled as I ran toward the car. "Call and report it."

Ten minutes later, we were in a rickety wooden cruiser heading as fast as it would go into a lake of fire.

This brought to mind a poetic phrase I'd heard somewhere, though I couldn't remember where or what it was from: Their portion will be in the lake that burns with fire and sulfur, which is the second death.

The rain continued to fall, but it had no visible impact on the fire.

The Liberty ship, adrift now in ever-expanding concentric

circles of flame, blazed before us, spreading its fuel and fire across the surface of the Gulf.

The inferno we were entering was so intense, so unimaginably hot, we could only navigate the edges.

The falling rain, the whining wind, the undulating sea, even the rolling, echoing thunder would not drown out the screams of the men shrieking in pain as their flesh melted from their bodies.

From within the ship came the horrific cries of the damned—tortured souls whose last moments were spent in unmitigated agony of apocalyptic proportions.

On deck, sailors caught fire as they ran toward lifeboats, leaping into the lake of fire below before realizing what they were doing.

One man was stuck in a porthole, his bottom half on fire, yelling for his mama with the unadorned abandon of a small, scared, suffering child.

We watched helplessly as the ropes holding a lifeboat burned in two, plunging sailors into the searing sea below.

"Circle around the perimeter," I yelled at the small Japanese man piloting the cruiser. "Get as close as you can."

We slowly trolled the waters, wiping rain from our eyes as we searched the burning, boiling Gulf for bodies.

The night was cold, the wind and rain adding to the low, miserable temperature, but nothing was a match for the intensity of the heat radiating from the hellish holocaust in front of us. I went from shivering on one side of the boat to sweating on the other.

We circled the site for nearly an hour, fishing seven men from the sea, most in their underwear having been in their bunk when the attack occurred, all wounded, all injured, all burned.

When we neared the marina, the two Japanese men who had earlier tonight been my captors jumped out of the boat and swam ashore and disappeared into the darkness.

Though she wasn't there, Bunko Matsumoto had help

awaiting our arrival at the dock and the wounded sailors were quickly loaded into ambulances and taken to the hospital.

From a pay phone on the far side of the marina I called Ruth Ann for a ride. When she pulled in to pick me up half an hour later I would have sworn it was Lauren behind the wheel.

As I got into the car I had a better view of the stunning transformation.

The clothes, the hair, the makeup, even the Paris perfume. Except for the blue eyes and lack of burns, I was sitting next to Lauren Lewis.

"Hey, soldier," she said. "You okay?"

I tried to speak but nothing came out.

"What is it, fella? You look like you've seen a ghost."

16

I woke up late the next morning feeling hung over, though I had had no liquor the night before.

I was sore and my head hurt—but neither were a match for the pain coming from beneath my seeping bandage.

Ruth Ann appeared at the doorway with a breakfast tray, looking even more like Lauren than the night before, her housecoat and matching slippers elegant and sexy in an understated way. Her hair and makeup were so perfect they could have been done by Lauren herself.

What did it mean? Should I say something? Wait for her to? Was she trying to comfort me, lessen my grief, or did she want to take Lauren's place somehow?

Without realizing what I was doing, I turned and looked at the photograph of Lauren to my right. This caused Ruth Ann to rush in and place the tray in front of me.

"How'd ya sleep, soldier?" she asked.

For now, I wouldn't say anything about her transformation.

"Huh? Ah ... good. Thanks. But that was my last night in your bed. I'm better now. You gotta take it back."

"You're not moving like you're much better," she said. "You

gotta stop making with all the nocturnal activities for a while, fella. What happened out there?"

I told her.

"Those poor boys."

I nodded, but didn't say anything, and we were silent for a few moments.

"How bad did you reopen your wound pulling those boys in the boat?" she asked.

"Not bad. I'm fine."

"I'll see for myself about that once you finish your breakfast. Eat up."

I pretended to, glancing at the paper on the tray as I did.

With the approach of Thanksgiving, the paper carried recipes and an article on how to prepare a wartime meal for the day, suggesting readers be flexible in making substitutions because many of the traditional items were scarce or unavailable. Turkeys were smaller because feed supplies were low. Many of the birds were being sent to soldiers overseas, so those of us on the home front were being asked to make due with chicken, which wasn't rationed, unlike red meat. If a chicken couldn't be found, we should try a pork shoulder. Instead of butter, we should use margarine or chicken or bacon fat. Sage, most of which came from Dalmatia, was unobtainable, so try using oregano in the dressing.

"What were you doing out there in the first place?"

I told her.

"I saw the picture in your coat. It got a little wet, but it's okay. Can't say the same for the ration stamps in your trouser pocket. They're ruined, but I got you some others."

She turned and took the picture of Miki Matsumoto off the dresser and studied it before handing it to me.

"She's a real looker," she said. "For a Jap."

"What do you know about the internment camps?" I asked.

"The what?"

I explained what I was talking about.

"I heard the Nazis had them. Didn't know we did. Oh, these were in your right-side coat pocket."

She grabbed several other items from the dresser and handed them to me.

The first was a flyer dated April 22, 1942 that read WESTERN DEFENSE COMMAND AND FOURTH ARMY WARTIME CIVIL CONTROL ADMINISTRATION, Presidio of San Francisco, California: INSTRUCTIONS TO ALL PERSONS OF JAPANESE ANCESTRY Living in the following area...

It detailed the procedures Bunko Matsumoto had mentioned to me.

The next was a book of matches with bombs falling on the front, with the caption Tokens for Tokyo like the one I had seen in the car Clip had stolen.

The final item was a button with a lapel pin that pictured two crossed rifles and said JAP HUNTING LICENSE. OPEN SEASON. NO LIMIT.

I shook my head.

"Come on, soldier, think about what they did," she said. "You're not gonna let some Jap skirt make you go all soft, are you?"

I didn't say anything, just handed her the tray.

"Sorry, fella. It's just ... think about how many of our boys at Pearl Harbor died just like the ones last night. Bombed to death. Burned alive. You saw hell firsthand. You know what I'm talking about."

I did.

I recalled thinking that very thing last night—that no wonder people conceived the worst possible punishment as burning alive for eternity. I hoped Lauren was right, that God was love and there was no such place as hell. Thinking of her in that kind of torment because of anything we had done made me want to set fire to the whole world. No, she had to be right. Humans created hell, not God. Hell is here and now, in inhumanity, in war and death, in loss, in the loss of Lauren. I was in hell. It was not awaiting me in the big beyond. It was my current condition. Here. Now. My ever present reality.

"I need to see the recent murder victims," I said. "Will your friend at the morgue show them to me?"

"Sure, soldier, he'll show 'em to you," she said. "As long as I tag along. We'll go right after I take a look at your wound and help you get dressed."

17

The morgue was dim, quiet, and cool.

Roy Nelson, a shy, socially awkward kid with pale skin and a boyish haircut with bangs that fell just below his eyebrows, snuck us in the back while his boss was at lunch. He was tall with black hair and eyes—the latter with enormous dark circles beneath them.

It was obvious he was smitten with Ruth Ann. It was equally and painfully obvious that though she didn't share his affection, she didn't mind exploiting it.

"Thanks again for helping us like this, Roy," she said. "It's awfully good of you."

He hesitated a moment before getting out, "Happy ... to ... help you, Ruth Ann."

He was leading us down a narrow corridor beneath the occasional bare bulb on a recently polished floor that squeaked intermittently under our feet as our shoes inadvertently scuffed it.

Roy walked very slowly, and I couldn't tell if it was his natural speed or if he did it out of consideration for Ruth Ann, who even with the good prosthetic leg was incapable of moving fast.

At one point he stopped and said, "I ... like the new way you're doin' your hair, Ruth Ann. It's real ... pretty."

"Thank you, Roy. Just trying something new."

He then led us into a room lined on both sides with a bank of corpse cold storage cabinets, a massive stainless steel monstrosity as cold and as impersonal as the lifeless shells it held.

My knees buckled a bit as I thought of Lauren's lifeless body lying in one of these while I was in a coma in a warm bed in another part of the sanatorium in Tallahassee, but I caught myself and didn't fall.

This is what it comes to, isn't it? Loss. And not just. Nothingness. Cold, inhuman nothingness. But is this all? Was Lauren waiting for me somewhere?

"Ruth Ann ... there's a room you can wait in right over here," Roy said. "There's a—"

"I'm not going anywhere, Roy."

"But ... you don't want to see this. No one ... who doesn't have to ... should ever see something like this."

"I'm sure it's bad, but I'm a war nurse. I'll be just fine."

"I'm not sure I will be," I said.

"This is after the violence," she said. "After the death and dismemberment. I saw it actually happen. Hell, it happened to me."

"Okay ... then. We'll do one at a time. And we can stop anytime. I ... I just ... want you to ... I'm just lookin' out ... for you."

"I know. Thank you, Roy. You're okay."

With that, he unlatched and swung open the first door and yanked on the tray, the body of a once beautiful young woman rolling out between us.

"This is the first victim," he said. "Janet Stewart."

Her ghostly skin was waxy white and bloodless, bisected at the waist, her two halves separated by six inches or so. The dark hair on her head and pubis provided a stark contrast to the unearthly paleness of her skin.

"Poor thing," Ruth Ann said.

"The way you see her here is about the way the body was discovered," Roy said. "No clothes. No blood. No marks. He cleans them up but good when he's finished cuttin' on them."

"Do you have copies of the crime scene photos?" I asked.

He looked at Ruth Ann.

She nodded.

"I can get 'em for you."

"Would you, Roy?" she said. "That would be so swell of you. I'd be so grateful."

I looked at her, gaining a new appreciation for this stranger who used to be my drinking pal not so very long ago. She was good. And a little scary.

"Probably take me a day or so."

"Just as soon as you can will be fine," she said. "Just fine."

He nodded. "Seen enough?" he asked.

I studied the body a bit longer, trying to take in everything I could, then indicated to him I had indeed seen enough.

As he rolled in the tray and closed the door, I asked Ruth Ann if she was okay.

She looked at me, our eyes locking, and I knew she was.

Roy said, "Can you believe Panama City has a sex killer?"

"It is hard to believe," Ruth Ann said.

As he opened the next door and pulled on the tray, he said, "He cuts a little more each time."

The second body looked nearly identical to the first—in body type, hair color, everything, even the method and manner of the murder and caring for the body afterward. The only difference was the right arm of this one had been cut off at the shoulder and it lay a few inches apart the same way the two halves above and below the waist did.

"They could be sisters," Ruth Ann said.

It was true, but I wondered how much of it had to do with their pale, washed-out, bloodless condition and what had been done to them. Had they looked this similar in life when what we were looking at now had been whole, with a heartbeat and blood and an embodied soul?

The final two were the same as the first—nearly exact in every way but with more and more cutting. The third victim was not only bisected but both arms had also been cut off. The fourth was bisected, had both arms and legs cut off.

Apart from being of Japanese descent, Miki Matsumoto bore a strong resemblance to the four girls killed so far, but she was not among them.

"Wonder how long before there's another?" I said.

18

Heaven Can Wait and Shadow of a Doubt were playing at the Ritz theater downtown, and though I paid my thirty cents to get in, I wasn't here to see either feature.

The Ritz stood next to the Tennessee House, not far from our old offices, and across the street from the police precinct. I was betting my freedom that I could blend into the wild nighttime crowd, but it was only a matter of time until I got spotted by the wrong person and the boys in blue threw the big net over me.

These were the chances I was taking. What other options did I have?

I was here to see a woman—a woman I was certain would not want to see me.

When Jan Christie wasn't working at the Ritz, she was one of nearly ninety volunteers coordinated by Warren Middlemas known as spotters, who took turns watching the sky for enemy aircraft from a station on top of the Dixie Sherman. Like the other volunteers, she had been trained to identify aircraft—both ours and theirs—by sight and sound.

The last time I saw her, what I thought would be the final time, I had seen her there on the roof of the Sherman.

When she had opened the door of the small wooden lookout shack and saw me standing there agitated and holding a brown paper bag, she shook her head.

"Not tonight, soldier," she said.

"But I brought your favorite," I said, holding up the whiskey.

"Every time she's close enough to get her poison in you," she said, "you show up here wantin' me to cut the wound open and suck out the venom."

She had been talking about Lauren and she had been right.

Although not nearly as beautiful or regal as Lauren, there was something about Jan that made me think of her. It was in her attitude, her posture, the hunger beneath her plaid skirt and white blouse. She was right. I only used her for temporary relief. Very temporary. And not just because I was so limited in what I could do. The next morning I would always feel far worse, my self-inflicted sickness and inexcusable cruelty toward a girl whose only sin was letting me, making me hate myself all the more.

She had closed the door and gone back to work. I had spread out my overcoat on the step, sat down, and started drinking.

I took a few pulls on the bottle and thought about what I was doing. I couldn't blame Lauren's power over me or Jan's weakness against me. I alone was responsible for the damage I was doing. I had become a carrier and was infecting her. I had to stop.

Standing up slowly, I had placed the bottle down on the step I had been sitting on and walked away. When I reached the exit door, I told her I was sorry and that I wouldn't be back, but I wasn't sure she heard it. And here I was back to see her, though for a very different reason.

The night I had called Pete with all the info on Frank Howell and the rest, I had gotten the impression that he was not alone. If I was right, then Jan was the most likely person whose presence I had detected. I hadn't been the only one who used Jan.

The Ritz theater was all right. There were always plenty of

people around—both inside and out—enjoying the pictures, sure, but enjoying each other more.

The manager, Bud Davis, was always finding ways to support the war effort, including hosting several war bond drives in front of the theater, which included special shows, demonstrations of amphibious vehicles, parades, and celebrities. He was even the one who came up with the slogan, "Your war bond may be his ticket home." He also hosted a free scrap metal movie and invited fourteen hundred boys and girls below the age of fourteen to donate a piece of scrap metal and see a free movie.

As I moved around the lobby looking for Jan, I avoided Bud and anyone else who might recognize me. It wasn't difficult to do. The crowd was active and talkative and easy to blend in to.

Unable to find Jan in the concession stand or lobby, I stepped inside the theater to look for her.

On the screen, Hitchcock's small-town malevolent master-piece was playing, the bright, innocent, but brilliant Charlie played by Teresa Wright telling her namesake uncle Charlie played by Joseph Cotten, "I have a feeling that inside you there's something nobody knows about ... something secret and wonder-ful. I'll find it out."

She's right about the secret part, but not the wonderful. I knew because I had read the story by Gordon McDonell, "Uncle Charlie," that the movie was based on.

I thought about how much I used to read, how little I had lately, and how much I missed it. I recalled using certain words I'd picked up from all my time between the covers, and July, Lauren, and Ruth Ann all having the same reaction—"You gotta get out more, fella, and stop reading so much. Have you heard yourself lately?"

Jan was walking up the aisle just a few feet away when she spotted me. She started shaking her head immediately and actu-ally stopped and took a step back.

I stepped toward her.

"Is there somewhere we can talk?"

"Stay away from me."

"It'll only take a minute. I swear."

"I'll scream."

"I'm not gonna hurt you. I just—"

"I mean it."

"Jan. Please. I'm trying to find Pete."

That stopped her.

"I just need a minute. Please."

Someone said, "Sit down, mister. I can't see the movie."

"Sorry, pal. I'm leaving."

"Meet me out front," she said.

"I can't be seen."

"I can't be alone with you."

"Back corner of the lobby?" I asked. "Or by the bathroom."

"Okay."

I walked out of the theater and back into the lobby and found the quietest, least conspicuous corner and waited.

I didn't have to wait long.

"Whatta you want, Jimmy?" she said as she walked up. "Aren't you wanted by the police?"

"Look," I said, "I haven't done anything. I'll get it all straightened out—or I won't. Doesn't matter. First thing I want to say to you is I'm sorry. I know I didn't treat you so good and I'm sorry. Real sorry. I was so messed up over Lauren ... That's not an excuse. I'm just saying ... I'm sorry."

"Is she really dead?"

"She really is."

"Can't say I'm sorry, but ..."

"No need to."

"So ... whatta you need from me, fella? I gotta get back to work."

"Pete's missing and I'm trying to find him."

"I don't know where he is. Haven't seen him in a while."

"How long a while? Were you with him the night I called and told him about Howell and the rest?"

She hesitated.

I could feel her wanting to say something, sense something coming up from within, so I waited.

"I ... Yes. I was there."

"What happened?"

"Whatta you mean?"

"Why didn't he go arrest them?"

"I thought he did," she said. "I mean, he was going to. When he left that's where he was headed."

"What happened?"

"I don't know. He never came back. I've never seen him again. It scared me but good too, soldier. He's a cop. I mean ... if something bad can happen to a cop ... And I know something bad happened, but there was nothing in the paper and no one seemed to know anything."

"No one knew anything at all? No theories? Ideas? Whispers?"

"Nothing."

"Any idea what he was working on before that night?"

"Two things. All those people beaten to death that you were suspected of ..."

"Did he really suspect me?"

"Yeah. He did. Some of the time, anyway. I think. Did you do it?"

"No," I said, shaking my head wearily. "I let him know who did when I called that night."

"So you didn't have anything to do with him going missing?"

"No. I didn't. I left town that night. I was in a coma and then a prisoner. I haven't been back long. Had no idea he was missing until just a few days ago."

She fell silent and seemed to think about it.

"What's the other thing?"

"Huh?"

"That he was working on?"

"Oh. Those girls that got cut up and killed."

"You sure? I thought those happened since he's been missing."

"I guess the others have, but I know he was at least working on the first one. Just thought it was the one at the time. It bothered him but good. I could tell."

"Anything else you can think of that might help me find him?"

She thought about it a moment then shook her head.

"Do you know if he went by himself? Did he take anyone? Call for backup? Talk to anyone at all?"

"He called his partner and asked for his help."

"Butch?"

"Yeah."

"You're sure?"

"Positive. When he left he was on his way to meet Butch."

19

P eople were hustling down Harrison—in cars on the street, by foot on the sidewalks—hanging out of the Tennessee House, in and out of shops, standing, smoking, walking, moving, talking.

Leaving the Ritz, I disappeared into the din, following the flow downstream, heading to Ruth Ann's car.

Rounding the corner at Fourth, I continued on toward Grace.

As I neared the car, I glanced down Fourth and saw a man angling onto Oak who I could've sworn was Cliff Walton.

He was a good distance away so I couldn't be certain, but his build and the way he walked were a perfect match for the man, except now he walked with a limp—a limp I had given him when I shot him in the leg the night I left town with Lauren.

Walt, as he was most often called, had been Harry Lewis's head of security, both for the bank and the campaign. He was a large man with a thick neck who wore suits a size or two too small for him. He was the type of man who entered a room a few minutes after his chest did.

On the night I shot him, I had not only discovered that he was actually working for Frank Howell as a plant pretending to work for Harry all the while blackmailing Lauren, but that he had killed a few people in the process.

He, Howell, Ann Everett, and Payton Rainer had been working together to use Lauren to get Harry to drop out of the race.

I hurried down Fourth then turned onto Oak hoping it was him and that he'd lead me to them, but Oak was empty and there was no sign of the figure I had seen limping down Fourth.

I stood there a moment trying to decide what to do.

About two blocks down, lights from a car parked on the side of the street came on and it pulled out onto Oak heading my direction.

I stepped back a bit and waited, and was glad I did.

As the car whisked past me, I could see that it was in fact who I thought it was. Cliff Walton, who helped killed Lauren, was not only still drawing breath, he was doing so right here in my little town.

So as the vehicle passed by, I stepped out into the street and carefully studied the tag so I could do something about it.

I walked back up Fourth toward Ruth Ann's car, salivating at the thought of seeing Walt again soon, savoring the unmitigated misery I was going to unleash onto his life.

Out in the bay, the Liberty ship still burned. Adrift. Aflame. Abandoned. Soon it would sink to the bottom and become a ghost ship—like me, a casualty of a war it never got to fight in.

As I turned from Fourth onto Grace and started to cross the street, the pristine Presidential Studebaker pulled up beside me.

Bunko Matsumoto's brother was in the backseat again, the same little driver in the front behind the wheel.

The door opened, I got in, and the driver pulled up and parked near the curb.

"Sister say ah you were ah interrupteda."

I nodded.

"How ah many boys you and my nephews save?"

"A few."

He nodded.

We were silent a moment, then he said, "Boat still ah burn out there ah right nowa. Beautiful in moonright."

"I went to the morgue this morning," I said. "Your niece is not one of the four girls cut up by the killer."

The release of stress and the relief that replaced it were palpable. His shoulders relaxed beneath his black suit coat and his breathing became more peaceful, less labored.

He rolled down his window a few inches, withdrew a red pack of Pall Mall that said WHEREVER PARTICULAR PEOPLE CONGREGATE, shook one out, and lit up without offering me one.

"So," he said, returning the pack to his pocket, "where is my niece then?"

"The only thing I know for sure is that she's not one of the madman's four victims in the morgue."

The smoke filling the car was strong and I decided to roll down my window—an awkward task accomplished by reaching over my body with my left hand and turning the knob at an odd angle the wrong way at first.

"You find her now."

"Right now?" I asked.

"Yes. Ah righta nowa."

"I don't know enough to even start. You want me to look for the girl, I'll look for her. And you don't have to threaten me to get me to do it. But you do have to give me some information. I gotta pick up her trail somewhere."

"Whata do you ah need ah to knowa?"

"The standard stuff," I said. "When she was last seen. With whom? By whom? Where was she? What was she doing? What was she supposed to be doing? What was she into? Who was she into? Did her behavior change in any way before she went missing? Stuff like that. Stuff you can't tell me. I want to talk to her best friend. And her boyfriend if she had one. And the sooner the better. The scent on that trail is growing fainter by the second."

20

"I checked on those sailors like you asked me to," Ruth Ann said.

"Thanks," I said. "How they doin?"

"Gonna make it.

I was in her room gathering my stuff when she walked in looking and sounding even more like Lauren. Had she been studying her? Looking at her pictures? Listening to the recordings of her? Reading her journals and letters?

Thinking of Lauren's letters made me want to read the one she left with Keller again.

"Twelve saved, all told. You saved half of 'em, soldier. What're you doing?"

"Packing up my stuff."

"What? Why? Where you goin'?"

"To the couch tonight. Out of your hair tomorrow."

"No," she said. "No need to shove. 'Sides, you're in no condition, fella. It's no good. Stay. Let me take care of you. It's no bother. I like having you here."

I continued to pack. Slowly. How I did everything these days.

I was slow enough without the arm, but the wound had worsened even that.

"Think about how much you're dealing with, soldier. Let me help you. I like helping you. I want to. Sleep on the sofa if you wanna, but don't leave. Besides, where would you go?"

Good question. I had no idea.

I placed Lauren's picture in the box with her letters and records and the other things I had of hers.

"I appreciate all you've done," I said.

"Am I doing something wrong?"

I shook my head. "But I feel bad for how much of a burden I've been, how much of your time and resources I've taken up."

"It's not a burden. I want to help you. Hell, I want you happy. I see how sad you are. I just want to make you happy. Let me help you. Let me make you happy."

As I fell asleep, I reread Lauren's letter again. Several times. Bits of it swirling around my head in the twilight between consciousness and sleep.

Meeting you has saved me. Being with you has caused me to wake up. Our love, mine for you and yours for me, has forever changed me.

This experience has been overwhelming for me, and I know I have not handled it well. I'm so very sorry for that. I know you've not understood and that you've felt betrayed, rejected, abandoned.

Please forgive me. Please know how very deeply I love you. Please don't ever stop loving me that same way.

Forgive me. Forgive Harry. Forgive yourself.

Quit trying to save the world.

There's so much more I want to say, but I'm out of time. You and I were always out of time, weren't we?

See you soon, my dear strong soldier.

All my love, all of me.

When I did fall fully asleep. I dreamt of her.

Lauren and I were making love in Margie's big bed. It was a foggy Friday morning, and we were entangled in a euphoria of sleepy sensual sex, the smell of her sending me, putting me in an altered state.

This was before. Back when Lauren was alive and Margie was alive and a friend to us, and let us use her place when Harry was in a board meeting or up to some other banking business neither of us cared a bit about.

We were saying things to each other that so many lovers before us had, so many after us would, but in our mouths they sounded like we were the first to say them, the only ones who ever would.

We felt like twins, two halves of the same soul, the same little piece broken off of the big all, that which was below and beneath and above and around. Love.

I was the god of her idolatry.

I had no god to commit idolatry on, so she was just my goddess.

I was hers. She was mine. Body and soul.

"I love your guts," she said.

"I adore every second, every inch, every breath, every beat of you."

I awoke with tears streaming out the corners of my eyes and into my ears.

I had agreed to stay a little longer at Ruth Ann's, but only on the couch, so when I opened my eyes, I was confused at first, disoriented, uncertain of where I was.

I looked around, remembering I was in Ruth Ann's living room.

What woke me up? What had I been dreaming?

And then I saw her. Lauren. Standing at the end of the sofa.

Her sheer robe was open, revealing her smooth, milky skin, the mound her dark hair in the inverted V the meeting of her legs made, the valley between her breasts, the nipples that pressed against and shone through the sheer.

"Lauren." I said her name like a supplicant's soft prayer in the darkness.

It really wasn't until she moved toward me and I saw her prosthetic leg that I had any idea it was Ruth Ann.

I started to sit up but she shoved me back, and she knelt down beside the sofa.

"I just want to make you happy, soldier," she said.

"Ruth—"

"Let me be her for you. I don't mind."

"You can't. I can't."

"We can. Let me show you."

She began pulling down my pajama bottoms and underwear.

"Ruth Ann," I said. "Stop."

"Just let me put you in my mouth. Let me show you how good I can be to you, how good we can be together."

She looked so good, and her hands on me, her body so close to mine, felt so good.

"It's no good," I said. "I couldn't if I wanted to. Remember?"

"Soldier, let me tell you a little secret. You can."

"Why are you—"

"I've been caring for you, fella, and I'm telling you you're just fine."

"What? What are you saying?"

"When you were out. When I bathed you. Every time I bathed you, you ... ah ... responded."

I couldn't believe it. What was she telling me?

"You can," she said. "We can."

I was so lonely, so sad, so wanted to be touched. Needed it. Could I let her be Lauren for me?

"I've always carried a torch for you, soldier," she said. "Always. I want you. I know you want her and I don't mind so much."

I could feel the warmth of her breath and skin, and her sleepy whispered voice was sweet and sexy at the same time. She looked and smelled like Lauren.

God, I missed her so much. Wanted her so bad. Needed her more than anything.

"Please," she said. "Let me heal you. I can make you feel good again. Let me show you."

And that's what did it. I didn't want to be healed, didn't want to feel better. I was miserable without Lauren, and though I didn't think anything could change that—not even a Lauren-like substitute—I didn't want to take that chance. I couldn't.

"I just can't," I said. "I'm sorry."

We sat there in silence a moment, breathing, being. Eventually, she laid her head down on me.

"Please don't be sore," I said. "Try to understand."

"You're a true romantic, soldier. I understand all too well. I'm not the least surprised. Lauren was one lucky girl. I just wanted a little of that. Not so much. Just one small little piece."

"Sorry."

"Plus I know I could make you happy."

"If anyone could ..." I said, letting it drift there between us. "And that's a chance I just can't take."

That seemed to give her some amount of comfort, and I was glad I said it.

21

The photographs were grainy, underlit, underdeveloped, utilitarian.

The contrast between them, between what was being captured and the way it was being captured, was stark and added to the overall unsettling nature of the images. It was as if a hack newspaper photographer was haphazardly snapping pictures of a Monet plein-air painting.

I was sitting up on Ruth Ann's couch flipping through the crime scene photographs, finding it difficult to do with one hand, awkward because it was my left.

The pictures were stacked in my lap atop the envelope they came in. They were 8x10s on thick, stiff paper. One at a time, I withdrew one from the stack, studied it, then placed it facedown next to me on the sofa.

They were in chronological order so I was moving from first victim to fourth, observing the killer's expansion and escalation.

Ruth Ann was in her bathroom getting ready. We had been eating breakfast when Roy brought the photographs by. It made him sore as hell that I was here and had obviously spent the night, but he didn't say anything, only seethed silently.

I was studying the pictures of the first victim, Janet Stewart, comparing what I had seen in the morgue with what I was seeing now.

She had obviously been a beautiful woman in life, and even after everything that had been done to her, she retained a certain bloom in death.

There was no blood.

Her skin was impossibly white.

Her dark hair was impossibly dark.

She was lying on black fabric that looked like satin.

The high contrast between the background and her body was severe and served to heighten the shocking impact of the image, and though the photograph was black and white, the subject matter was such that it would've looked the same at the scene.

Her legs were spread open, her feet extended up and out. There was something subtly but decidedly sexual about the pose. Above her legs, the top half of her bloodless bisected body was only a few inches away, but had not been lined up precisely, so the two parts were slightly askew.

Her arms were up, one draped over her eyes, as if sleeping while shading from a bright light, the other bent so that her hand fell gently between her breasts.

As I moved to the second victim, I realized I only had the name of the first one. None of the victims' names had yet been released, so none were in the paper, and if Roy had mentioned any but the first's name, I didn't recall.

The second body was also posed on the black satin material and looked nearly identical to the first—except in addition to being bisected, the right arm had been cut off at the shoulder. The positioning of the body was different as well.

This time, the bottom half of the body was turned over, the knees up and out, raising the buttocks as if preparing for rear entry or anal sex. The top half remained facing up, but there was more room between the two parts. The left arm that was still attached was extended straight out, while the detached right arm was several inches from the place where it had been severed, at a ninety-degree angle, hand open, palm up.

Displayed on the same cloth, the bloodless body prepared in the same pristine manner, the third victim was not only bisected but both arms had also been cut off. This time, the torso was facedown and the bottom half was up. On top of her pubic bone, just above the dark triangle of curly, coarse hair, her crossed arms formed an X.

Finally, the fourth was bisected and had both arms and both legs cut off.

Splayed out wide on the black satin with nearly a foot between each section, the pale parts of the young woman formed a cadaver crucifixion—arms stretched out wide, hands closed into fists of pain, legs straight down, feet pointing down, crossed at the ankles.

After studying each image over and over again, I returned to the very first impression I had upon seeing the very first photograph. The contrast between what was being captured and the way it was being captured was jolting. The photographs were serviceable at best, but their subjects were something else entirely.

The killer was creating art. The photographer was merely making a record.

It made me wonder what a photographic artist could have done, and I felt certain the killer had created artistic renderings of his work—drawings, paintings, photographs, films. Something. Some way to savor it.

"Well?"

I looked up.

Ruth Ann was standing there.

"Well?" she said again. "What do you think?"

"There's something there," I said. "Something about them...

reminds me of something I've read or seen, but I just can't quite ... If I had my books ..."

"I thought you did," she said, glancing over at the boxes in the corner of the room.

"My office at the agency and my room at the Cove were full. That's just a few of them."

"I can help you get them."

"No need. I know who to ask. But there is something you can do."

"Name it."

"Will you see if you can get the names of all the victims from Roy? Where they were found. Anything else he knows about them. And I'd also really like to see pictures of them from when they were alive if there's any way."

"I'm on it."

22

"You gotta good eye, sugga," Mama Cora said. "'Specially for a dead man."

She was flipping through the crime scene photographs, smoke from her long ivory churchwarden pipe swirling around her.

I wasn't sure what all was in the pipe, but I knew it wasn't just tobacco.

"They're artistic, right?" I said. "I mean, he's creating something, experimenting maybe. Definitely displaying, exhibiting."

"Yes, yes, yes, yes, yes. Now give Mama a minute to look at them."

Mama Cora was a three-hundred-pound Creole woman with light caramel skin and closely cropped rust-colored hair—most of which was hidden beneath a colorful silk do-rag. She had bohemian sensibilities, which were reflected both in the gypsy way she dressed herself and the artistic way she decorated her house.

The explosion of color inside the small house off Cherry Street was so intense it was too much to process. Bright yellows and brilliant aqua blues, oranges and limes, pinks and purples on rugs and walls, furniture, screens, hanging beads, and works of art.

Mama Cora wore a silk teal wrap with pink and gold and purple designs. She had rings on every finger, several in each ear, and one in her nose.

"Sit down, honey," she said. "Give Mama a second to study these."

I stumbled onto a too low stack of pillows that were less stable than they even appeared and waited.

The stunningly beautiful and talented daughter of a French-African woman and a white man, Cora had toured and lived in most of the world as a singer and dancer when she was younger, including France, Germany, and England. A born student and collector, she had an insatiable appetite for information, knowledge, wisdom, art, and artifacts. She knew more about most things than anyone I knew.

"Why does Dada come to mind?" I asked.

She smiled her enormous smile, her chubby cheeks rising, her eyes narrowing. Her teeth were big and blindingly white, the front two with a gap the size of a matchstick between them.

"Soldier boy done been usin' his library card again. Good on you, baby. Dada's not quite right but it's close. It inspired what inspired this."

"Oh yeah? What's that?"

"Anti-war, anti-bourgeois movement. Began in Switzerland during World War I. Involved art, literature, visual arts. Was a rejection of the norms and standards of the time. Included some anarchy. Was meant to point out the meaninglessness of the modern world."

I nodded, tying to recall anything I could about the movement.

"This cat here is a surrealist—or inspired by them. And surrealism was influenced by Dada."

"So surrealism is ..."

"Can be anything, baby," she said. "Art, literature, philosophy —anything stressing the subconscious, the non-rational, imagery arrived at by automatism, chance, unexpected juxtapositions."

"Automatism?"

"Automatic writing or drawing," she said. "Kinda like improvisational jazz for visual artists."

I nodded.

"It's been flourishing in Europe," she added. "Now, with so many them poor folk fleeing Europe, it's taking root here. Dada produced works of anti-art, deliberately defying reason, but not surrealism. No. Surrealism emphasizes not the negation as Dada did, but the positive—artistic expressions that challenge, not destroy. It's a reaction against rationalism, a means of reuniting conscious and unconscious, dream and fantasy."

I sat there silent for a moment, balancing on the pillows, thinking about what she had said.

"Let Mama show you, sugga," she said, grunting as she struggled to get up. "I got some examples 'round here somewhere. You'll see what I mean."

It took a while, but she finally found some loose leaf drawings and a bound book or two with images that illustrated everything she had been telling me, and I could see why with even as little as I had known, something in my subconscious had linked the work of the killer and the artists in the movement.

The surreal images she showed me were filled with a variety of female body parts and partial female bodies, nearly all of which were melted and misshapen, oblong and elongated. Many of them were mixed with parts of animals and elements of nature, but some were neither distorted nor mingled with other objects—just pieces and parts of the female form that closely resembled, in style and sensibility at least, the crime scene photographs.

We finished looking at everything surrealist she had, she

agreed to let me borrow a couple of books, and as was her custom she was walking me to the door to hug and kiss me goodbye.

"So we've got a ripper-like killer making art out of his victims," I said. "He could be from Europe, but wherever he's from he's either a surrealist or influenced by them."

"I'd say that about sums it up, sugga," she said. "Let me ask around a little and see what else—"

She stopped in midsentence as she opened the door and Butch was standing there, gun drawn, huge, mean smile on his face.

23

"I knew you'd come see that fat nigger bitch eventually," Butch said.

We were in his car, and though I wasn't sure where we were heading, I knew where we weren't. The station was in the opposite direction.

He was driving. I was in the front passenger seat.

Handcuffing a one-armed man is a difficult thing to do, so Butch had one cuff around my left wrist and the other through the metal cage behind us, so my arm was suspended awkwardly above my head.

"You're a real genius," I said.

"This ain't gonna go so well for you, pal, but keep up with the mouth and it'll go even worse."

I shook my head.

"You're too crooked to know it, but I'm a good cop. The whole force is looking for you, but I found you."

"The hell we goin'?" I said. "If you were a good cop, you'd be taking me to the station."

"If you'd've just killed all those civilians, I'd take you in and let you take your chances, but no way you kill my partner and not put the big snuff on you myself."

"The hell you talkin' about, Butch? I don't care how good you think your frame job is, nobody's gonna believe I killed Pete. He was my partner first. Would still be if I hadn't gotten my arm blown off."

"Save it, pal. You ain't gonna work me."

"I'm not trying to work you. I'm just talking to you. Telling you—"

"You're gonna do plenty of talking by the time I get done with you—only you're gonna once in your entire worthless goddamn life tell the truth."

I didn't respond and we bounced along in his old black cop car in silence for a while.

"I ain't gonna lie to you," he said. "You're goin' down for what you done, but you can save yourself a lot of ... ah ... unpleasantness by just comin' clean."

"You serious? Come clean about what? What is it you think I've done?"

"Okay. Play it that way, pal. Only don't forget you had a chance to save yourself a hell of a lot of misery."

He seemed sincere, like he really believed I was guilty. Could that be? If he were just trying to cover up crimes he had committed, why try to get me to confess? When I had dealt with him before, I had believed he was corrupt, looking to set me up, covering his ass if not his crimes, but now I wasn't so sure. Maybe he wasn't corrupt so much as incompetent.

"Butch, I have no idea what happened to Pete," I said. "I wasn't even in town at the time. Did something happen you're trying to cover up, or do you really not know?"

"You sure you don't wanna start singing? Your old hotshot Pinkerton partner ain't around to save your ass no more."

"You're right. He's not. And you know why? Because I shot him in self-defense. That's what I was doing the night Pete disappeared. That and driving to Tallahassee with Lauren Lewis for medical treatment. I crashed my car into Johnston's Sanatorium. Check it out. It's true. I've shot only three people lately: Stanley Somerset, Cliff Walton, and Ray Parker. Somerset and Walton only got a limp out of the deal. Ray is the only one in the ground. All of them dealt the play. All were self-defense on my part."

"Pretty story, pal. You should sell it to the pictures."

He drove me out to a secluded area in the middle of the woods.

We walked through the woods to a small clearing under the bright light of the afternoon sun, the cool wind pleasant, the day peaceful and pretty. Was this the day that was to be my last? I wouldn't mind so much—but I'd like to find Pete and to bring justice to Lauren's killers first.

The little clearing was the same spot Butch had brought Ray to when he was going to shoot him after Ray retaliated for Butch's bullying—which resulted in Butch's fat ass on the ground.

It was the site of an old moonshine still.

Butch had been part of a group of cops who discovered it and busted it up here in the pinewoods near Sandy Creek.

Since moonshine had soared in price, stills had sprouted up all over the Panhandle. Even employees of Wainwright Shipyard with good jobs were quitting to become ridge runners instead. This was one of the many all around us, one of the few that had been found and destroyed.

Nothing original about Butch, he led me to the exact same spot he had Ray, and made me kneel down in the exact same position in front of the same open well.

The hand-operated pitcher pump connected to the shallow well was still here—along with the various metal vats and buckets, hoses and hardware, and what was left of the overturned and smashed barrels.

He had cuffed my wrist to my ankle and had his gun pressed

against the back of my head. He was going to shoot me in the head and dump my body in the well.

"Spill," he growled.

I didn't say anything.

"Where's Pete? What'd you do with him?"

I still didn't respond.

"Tell me where he is and I won't kill you. I swear it."

He paused, but continued quickly when I remained quiet.

"Look, he's my partner. I've got to find him. Even if he's dead. I can't just leave him out there somewhere. Not know. You know that. Hell, he was your partner before he was mine. You know how these things work. How they got to be."

"Tell you what," I said—but before I could say anything else, I heard a loud crack and Butch fell forward on top of me.

24

W hen Butch opened his eyes and saw Clip standing beside me, he shook his head.

We had him propped up on the side of the well and had just splashed water in his face.

Spitting and letting out a mean burst of humorless laughter, he said, "A one-armed dick and one-eyed nigger. If that just don't beat all."

Clip's gun was drawn, the same one that cracked the back of Butch's skull a few minutes before, and was pointed at him. I was holding Butch's gun, but not pointing it directly at him.

"You gonna kill another cop?"

"You no more a cop than I is," Clip said. "You bent as hell. Badge don't change that."

"What happened to Pete?" I said.

"You tell me."

"Butch, I wouldn't be asking you if I knew where he was or what happened to him."

"Yeah? Well ... me neither."

He had a point.

"I told you where I was and what I was doing when Pete went missing," I said. "Return the favor."

"Go fuck yourself."

Clip thumbed back the hammer of his revolver.

"Butch, the night I left town, I called Pete and gave him evidence against Howell and his helpers. That's the last I spoke to him. But the person who was with him said he called you after that. What'd he say?"

"To meet him at Howell's."

"And?"

"And I did. And there was no one there and he never showed. 'Cause you killed them all."

"How long'd it take you to get there?"

"Long enough for you to take 'em out I reckon. And your nigger to clean up the mess."

I shook my head.

"You ain't gonna get away with it," he said. "Even if you fade me. Whole force is looking for you. You don't get away with killin' cops. You just don't."

"Why're we having this conversation?" I asked.

"Huh?"

"If I killed Pete and the others—by the way, whatta you think made me do that?"

"There's talk, buster. You took Lewis's wife. You were squaring whatever they done to her."

"So if that's true—and all I'm doing now is covering it up— why we talking? Why am I asking you about Pete? Why am I trying to find him if I know where he is? Why am I trying to find out what happened to him, if I already know?"

He had nothing for that.

"You got nothin' to lose by tellin' me the truth," I said.

He didn't say anything.

"Okay, but if I find out you had anything to do with Pete, we'll come for you—and there won't be any talking then. Just the big sendoff."

I turned and started walking away. Clip followed—walking backward at first, then when far enough away, turning.

"That's it?" Butch said.

I stopped walking and turned toward him.

"You not gonna punch my ticket?"

"I'll leave your gun at the end of the road," I said.

I turned and started walking again, catching up to Clip who hadn't stopped but had slowed. "I don't understand," Butch said.

We kept walking.

"Wait," he yelled.

We stopped walking and he caught up to us.

"You're really gonna let me live?"

"Yeah," Clip said. "That punishment enough."

"Why?"

"'Cause you a miserable fat—"

"No," he said to Clip, then turning to me said, "Why you gonna let me live?"

"I've been truthful with you," I said. "I'm just trying to find out what happened to Pete."

"Me too," he said, and we continued walking.

The twin trail path we were on was an old dirt logging road that had grown over. Above us, the sky was clear, the sun bright. Beneath us, the brownish grass was sun-dappled, the path criss-crossed with the elongated shadows of midsize pines.

After a short way, Butch began breathing heavily, his shirt soaked through, though the day was cool.

"That was the night we found the second victim," he said between labored breaths. "I was on my way to meet Pete when I got radioed about it. I was told to go directly to the crime scene, that Pete was being told the same thing, that it took precedence. Everything else would have to wait. I did as I was told. After a while, when Pete didn't show up, I rushed over to Howell's and found it empty. Just like I said."

"You think he tellin' the truth?" Clip asked.

We were on our way back into town. He was driving. I was thinking.

"Now don't get carried away," I said. "I doubt he could ever do that, but there might be less lies than usual in what he's saying."

He nodded, a small smile twisting on his large lips, but didn't say anything.

Lena Horne was singing "Stormy Weather" on the radio, and it made me think of Lauren and miss her even more. Of course, everything made me think of her, and maybe I really couldn't miss her any more than I did, but there it was.

"Like you to keep following him for a while if you can," I said.

"You keep payin', I keep followin'."

"And keep your eye out for Cliff Walton. I saw him downtown last night."

"You think Howell and the others still around too?"

I shrugged. "Be strange they didn't all leave town, but ... maybe they sent him back."

"Maybe he da one shootin' at your ass. Got the priest instead."

"May be."

"He walkin' with a limp these days?"

"A wicked one," I said.

He smiled appreciatively. "You Dillinger as hell, my man. Dillinger as hell."

25

With Clip following Butch and keeping an eye out for Walt, and Ruth Ann finding photographs and information about the four victims, I was at the beach.

It was evening, and the soft gold glow of the descending sun cast a dreamlike quality over everything.

The green waters of the Gulf were spiky, sea-foamed and white-capped, the sea oats clustered on the dunes waving in the wind.

Calm.

Peaceful.

Airy.

The beach was empty for miles in every direction—those who just came for sunning and swimming in the summer missing out on one of the best experiences the beach had to offer. Sunsets in the approach of winter solstice.

But I wasn't here to take in the breathtaking beauty of the setting sun. I was here to talk to Rina, a young Japanese woman who was not only Miki Matsumoto's best friend, but the last person to see her before she went missing.

I didn't know much about Rina, not even her last name, but

what I observed was a pretty, if plain, young woman who was calm, composed, and spoke better English than I did.

"Were you locked up with the others at Manzanar?"

"I was."

"Well, I can see why. It's obvious you pose a great threat to this country."

She gave no indication she knew I was being sarcastic.

I turned and glanced at the young guy who had driven me out here to meet her, and when I looked back I caught her staring at what was left of my right arm.

"I wasn't in the war," I said.

She acted flustered, embarrassed.

"It's okay," I said. "I just wanted you to know. I was a police officer. It got blown off here. I never served."

"I am sorry. I—"

"Don't be."

"It is just ... how do you do ... detective work with only one ... arm?"

"Same way I do most things. Slowly and awkwardly. And not very well."

"I am sorry. I should not have asked."

"It's fine. Really. Would you tell the driver I said to wait in the car?"

I turned as she spoke to him in Japanese, and he glared at me, our eyes locking, though he continued to speak angrily to her.

"He says he will not go anywhere."

"Tell him I said if we cannot speak in private we will not speak at all, and he can be the one to explain that to Bunko and her brother."

I was still staring at the guy, but from the corner of my eye I could see her give a slight bow.

"Very well," she said, then spoke to him in Japanese again—and he, her. "He will walk a bit away, but he will not let me out of his sight."

"It's his hearing not his sight that's the issue."

She said something else to him and he began to back away, watching us the entire time.

"He says if you try anything at all he will kill you."

"Tell him back at him."

She told him and he laughed and held up his thumb and forefinger in the shape of a gun, shot me, blew on the barrel, then holstered it.

"Let me guess," I said. "He likes American Western movies."

"Yes."

"And the only thing he understands is the shooting."

She didn't respond.

While I waited for him to get far enough away, I looked out across the sand and sea again to the setting sun, now a shimmering red-orange crest half hidden by the horizon.

When the gunman was at least twenty feet away, I nodded to her.

"I am not sure what I have to tell. Just that Miki was a good girl. Sweet and kind. The best friend I ever had."

"I'm sure she was, but I need to know anything you know that can help me find her. Do you know where she is?"

"She was always happy and looking for fun and excitement. She was very carefree, maybe even a little careless, but she had no guile, nothing but goodness in her. Her mother is so overbearing, so overprotective, so over everything, but even with that Miki mostly just obeyed."

"I don't need to hear about her obeying. I need to know the ways she disobeyed. I only care about finding her. I'm not going to look for her any less if she didn't always obey. Understand?"

She seemed to think about it for a long time, then nodded.

"I only want to find her. Nothing else matters to me. I don't care what she's done, who she's with, or why she left."

"There is a little motel not far from here. We would sneak down there sometimes. The night clerk is a sweet boy. Makes us drinks. We listen to music. Talk. Dance. Laugh. We laughed so much." I nodded, encouraging her to continue.

"That is where we were the night she disappeared. I do not want to get in trouble and I do not want to get her in trouble. I just want her to be okay."

"What happened?"

"There was this soldier. Passing through. He was cute. He hung out with us. We drank and talked and ... he liked Miki and she liked him. I could tell. He asked her back to his room and to my surprise she went. That left me and Paul—that is the night manager's name—but soon I realized he didn't care to hang out with just me. I guess all along he liked Miki too. Anyway, I walked back here—well, to the place we all hide out in. I think what she did was shameful, but she is not a shameful person, Mr. Riley. I thought she would come back later that night, but I guess she never did. The next morning she was missing. I guess she never came home."

"Have you told anyone?"

"No, sir. I tried to, but I just ... Can you go get her back without anyone ever knowing what she did or that I knew?"

26

The Magnolia Motor Court on the west end of Panama City Beach had eight yellow bungalows in a U shape built around a common area in the middle with landscaping in need of serious attention. Each bungalow had green trim and individual porticos and awnings.

It appeared the once nice motor lodge had suffered greatly during the war the way so many things had—especially tourist and travel-related businesses.

At the turn of the century, there were only about eight thousand registered automobiles in America. By 1930, that number had exploded to some twenty-three million. It looked as though the Magnolia Motor Court had been built in the 30s and probably did quite well until the start of the war. The night was cold and windy, the planted palms clacking and flapping in the brisk breeze when I walked into the front office of the motel beneath the green sign in the shape of an M.

"Hiya, soldier. Need a room for the night?"

"You Paul?"

He hesitated, the warm, open face he had greeted me with closing, growing suspicious.

"Ah ... yeah. Yes. Why?"

He had blond hair and greenish eyes, a round boyish face with pale skin splotched with light pink patches.

He added, "How do you know my—"

"I'm looking for Miki Matsumoto."

"Oh," he said, seeming to relax again. "I see. You with the government?"

"Why do you ask that?"

"Well ... you're ah ... arm. And ... the fact that she ... ah ... ran off with that soldier."

"You're awful friendly with the enemy," I said.

"Miki and Rina? They're just girls. They're not dangerous, are they?"

"What's his name?" I said.

"Who?"

"The soldier. Let me see where he signed in."

"Gee, mister, I don't know if I oughtna do that."

"You oughtna," I said.

"But—"

"A young girl is missing, son. We don't have time for this. Show me where the soldier signed in or I'll arrest you for obstructing justice."

He hesitated for just a moment, then turned the sign-in book toward him, flipped one page back, found the name, and turned it back toward me with his index finger on it.

I looked at it.

Miles Russet. 176 Gray Avenue, Mobile, Ala. 36601.

"What can you tell me about him?"

"He and Miki hit it off. And in a hurry."

"That bother you?" I asked. "What I hear, you were pretty sweet on her yourself."

"No sir. I mean, I like her, but not really like that. A little, maybe, but ... well, two things ... I couldn't be with a girl that likes a fella like him ... and well, I couldn't be with a Jap girl. My parents would kill me."

I nodded. "What was wrong with the soldier?"

"Loud. Arrogant. Obnoxious. It surprised me out of her. But she's young and he was in uniform. Nothing to get my pulleys tangled up about."

"You know where he was headed? Back to Mobile or—"

"Camp Gordon Johnston and boy was he dreading it. Wouldn't surprise me none if he took the girl away and went AWOL."

Camp Gordon Johnston, known as Hell by the Sea, was a one-hundred-sixty-five-thousand-acre military training camp near Carrabelle—about fifty miles from Tallahassee.

Opened in 1942, when the War Department was challenged with finding amphibious training bases with favorable year-round climate, Camp Gordon Johnston stretched some twenty-one miles along the coast and included Dog Island, St. George Island, and the area around Alligator Harbor.

Though very little official information came out of the camp, even though it published a newspaper called the Amphibian, it had a reputation as one of the most difficult training facilities in the entire country, attempting, and many would say succeeding, at creating the harsh conditions of war.Sand-floor tents, bad meals eaten standing up, outdoor latrines, horrible odors, sliding under barbed wire carrying their weapons, machine gun rounds flying overhead, planted charges exploding all around, snakes slithering around everywhere, chiggers, ticks, and swarms and swarms of yellow and dog flies and hoards of mosquitos—this was Camp Gordon Johnston.

"Can I borrow your phone?" I asked.

"Sure. Why?"

I didn't respond, and he placed the phone on the counter and turned it toward me.

I dialed the number Harry had given me. He had said he'd

help me any way he could. I was about to put that to the test. I was also about to see just how much juice he really had.

"Hello?"

Harry sounded sleepy, as if I had woken him up.

"I need to find out if a soldier is at Camp Gordon Johnston and if he is, I need to talk to him. You got enough credit for something like that?"

"Jimmy?"

"Yeah."

"Sure, fella. I can do that. How soon?"

"Now."

"Okay," he said, clearing his throat, trying to sound more awake. "Who's the soldier?"

I told him.

"He have something to do with Lauren's ... with what happened to Lauren?"

"Could," I said.

"Call you right back. Tell me where."

Half an hour later, Ruth Ann and I were driving along the coast beneath a bright low-slung moon, racing toward Carrabelle and Camp Gordon Johnston.

We were in her car, but I was driving. Lights on low beams, the top half blacked out, providing very little illumination on the dim, desolate highway.

Bing Crosby was singing "Moonlight Becomes You" on the radio, while through the right-side window, the bright moon bathed the Gulf in shimmering liquid pearl that seemed to sparkle and fix effervescently.

We rode along in silence for a long time, listening to the radio, looking at the rural road and the magnificent Gulf, which even at night was truly something to see.

Eventually, I took the opportunity to broach the subject of her transformation again.

"Do you know how many times I've started to call you Lauren?" I said.

"Really?" she said, feigning surprise and suppressing the obvious pleasure that it brought her.

"Why the change?"

"I told you."

"Tell me again."

"I know how much you miss her."

I didn't say anything.

"You do miss her something terrible, don't you, soldier?"

"More than my right arm."

"I thought so. So I thought why not ... you know ... bring her back. Look like her a little. I don't mind. I don't care how I look. Never have. I'm happy to do it for you, fella. Really I am. I know what it's like to love someone that much that you can't have."

"But I miss you too," I said. "My drinking buddy. My kid sister with the blond flip-out."

She looked down and nodded. "I know," she said softly. "I just ..."

"What?"

She didn't say anything.

"You just what?"

"I just don't want to be your kid sister no more, soldier."

That one hurt. I knew the way she felt. Hell, who hadn't experienced the exact same thing. Two people going along as friends and then one of them decides they don't want to be friends anymore, but the other doesn't feel the same. There was nothing to be done for it, nothing I could say or do, and my heart hurt for her. And it wasn't just that I couldn't love her that way. I could never love anyone that way but Lauren. Not now. Not ever.

27

We met with Miles Russet in a room in the old Lanark Inn, which had been used as the temporary headquarters when the camp originally opened.

East of Carrabelle, the Lanark Inn began operation as a seaside resort in the 1890s. Accessible by road from Tallahassee or Carrabelle and by rail on the Georgia Railroad, the inn catered to luxurious living, boasting an "extraordinary pure spring," gas lights, spring beds, hair mattresses, a two-hundred-foot porch, dancing pavilion, a long dock, and an enclosed swimming area where bathers were protected from sharks.

The inn burned down in the 1930s but was rebuilt in time to serve as the original Camp Gordon Johnston headquarters and later the nurses' quarters.

The "extraordinary pure spring" that had been one of the main attractions of the old hotel had been capped, its water flow diverted for use in the camp's sewerage facilities.

We had been allowed through the military police shacks along Highway 98 and allowed to drive through to the old inn, showing just how much power and influence Harry really had—

and this having little or nothing to do with him now being mayor of Panama City.

Hell by the Sea wasn't only used for amphibious training, but had just this year become the home to the Pigeoneer Department under the 4th Engineer Special Brigade's 828 Signal Corps. Pigeons carried messages, maps, and photographs in tube-and-saddle devices fastened to their backs. Traveling between thirty and seventy-five miles per hour, they could fly as many as six hundred miles in a day between first light and dark. They were even used in aircrafts, released at some twenty thousand feet from planes, in paper bags that helped protect them from the initial plunge.

Miles Russet was about as average as a body could be. Average build. Average height. Average looks. His nondescript uniform only adding to the averageness of his appearance.

We were seated in a small room off the main lobby, Russet and I across from each other at a large wooden desk, Ruth Ann behind me and to my right, pretending to take notes.

"That's my second biggest fear," he said, nodding toward my missing arm. "I'm most afraid of dying like everybody else, you know? But second to that is to come back with bits of me blown off. How'd it happen?"

"You stayed at the Magnolia Motor Court in Panama City Beach a couple of nights ago," I said.

He didn't say anything at first. "Ah, yeah. Why?"

"Who'd you stay with?"

"Huh? Nobody. Had my own room."

"Who stayed with you?"

"Was just me."

"We know that's not true," I said.

"Whatta you mean, fella? I swear it was just me."

"Look, pal, you can level with us and we'll be on our way or you can keep lying and we'll FUBAR your life. And I mean but good. Got it? Now tell me who was with you in your room?"

"Nobody. Honest. I swear."

"Do you know a Miki Matsumoto?"

"A what?"

"A young Japanese girl named Miki Matsumoto."

"Oh. I thought you meant a real person. Sorry, sir. I wasn't lying to you. Honest I wasn't. What's that little Jap whore sayin'?"

"Where is she?"

"Whatta you mean? How would I know?"

"Where'd you take her?"

"Back to my room for just a few minutes. She didn't stay long at all. Little Jap bitch was just a tease. You know the type, soldier."

With that he glanced over at Ruth Ann for the first time then quickly back to me. "Anyway. Nothing happened. She faded but fast and I hit my rack. I swear on my mother's life that's the truth."

"Was there anything in his room?" I asked. "Anything at all— left by him or her—that might help me figure out what happened or where she went?"

I was back at the Magnolia Motor Court after dropping Ruth Ann back at her place when we returned from Carrabelle.

"Well, gee, mister, I haven't even been in it yet," Paul said. "We're kinda slow right now. Figured I'd clean it by the week's end."

"Can I look at it?"

"Sure," he said. "I'll go with you."

He grabbed a key off a hook on the board behind him, and I followed him out into the night.

The breeze was less brisk, but still strong, and the temperature had dropped even more. Clouds shrouded the moon and from somewhere a shudder banged against the boards beneath it, a continuous, monotonous knocking like a persistent visitor in the middle of the night.

"Guess I should've checked the room before now," he said.

I looked around at the vacant motor court.

"Anybody staying here tonight?"

He shook his head. "Not at the moment."

Nothing around us for miles. We could be the only two people on the planet—a thought made more disturbing by the wicked whine of the wind and the slapping of the shudder.

When he unlocked and opened the door, he reached in and slid his hand up to turn on the light, then stood aside to let me enter.

What I stepped into was a small but immaculate old room that smelled a little stale and musty.

"Huh," he said behind me. "Guess Joe must've cleaned it when I wasn't here. I didn't realize."

"Who?"

"My boss. The day manager."

"You sure this is the right room?"

"Well yeah. I rented it to them myself."

"Them?"

"I mean him. He rented the room. Didn't bring her back 'til later. Became their room I guess."

"Smells like it's been a while since anybody was in here."

"All our rooms smell like that. No matter what we do. We can't get that old air smell out of 'em. They've just set up too long. I could ask Joe if he found anything when he comes in."

I nodded. "Thanks. Do you mind if we look in every room? Just for my—"

"Sure. I don't mind. Got nothing else to do. Let me grab the keys."

"That's not a master?"

He shook his head. "'Fraid not. I'll be right back."

He dashed away and I waited, wondering if Russet had told the truth, and if Miki Matsumoto had really left his room early and on her own, where she went.

When Paul got back, we began searching the place room by room.

Every room was more or less identical, and each time, as if a ritual, he would unlock and open the door, turn on the light, stand aside, and let me enter.

When he did it on the fourth room we looked in, cabin 5, the light didn't come on at first.

When it finally did flicker on to offer a dim, ghostly greenish glow, I found what I was seeing shocking, but not surprising.

There, spread-eagle on the bed, wrists and ankles tied, blindfold over her eyes, gag in her mouth, Miki Matsumoto was naked, dried blood between her thighs, on the sheet between her legs, and crusted in her nostrils.

"She was alive when you were out here earlier," he said.

And then ... blow to the back of the head, knees buckling, body pitching forward, unconscious before I hit the floor.

28

"Goddamn Jap bitch," he said, looking over at her. "Who the hell has you looking for her?"

He had me tied up in the bathroom, my arm bound to my body by a thick grass rope wrapped around me several times, my feet bound at the ankles. He had dumped me in the tub, my head next to the faucet. Beyond him through the door, I could see Miki's body on the bed. I was dazed and weak, and he had me tied up but good. I didn't see any possible way out of the situation. I was about to die in the bathtub at a roadside motor court in the middle of nowhere. How had I let this happen?

My head was full of snakes and they were crawling.

"Who all knows she even came here?" he said. "I guess that other Jap cunt is running her mouth to beat the band. Goddamn it."

He had a large kitchen knife, which he waved as he spoke, looking wild-eyed back and forth between me and the girl as he did.

He kept talking, but I wasn't listening. It was all I could do to think.

I thought about how if I died tonight I would have failed not only to save Lauren, but to settle things with those who helped rip her from this life she so loved.

I thought about how many people had tried to kill me, how many still were. Would I really die by the hand of this splotchy-faced boy? I had been shot, stabbed, had my arm blown off, withstood torture by a blonde Nazi bitch. I had survived a struggle to the death with the legendary Ray Parker, former Chicago cop and Pinkerton, and now a motel clerk was going to be the one to finally do it, finally finish me off.

I thought about how inept I was, how bad I was at this job I was doing, this type of work that had been the only type of work I had ever really done as an adult. And it wasn't just that I was wounded and dismembered, but to let happen what just happened, to let a little weak blond boy get me in such a position showed just how compromised mentally I was these days. Was it these days? The loss of Lauren and the rest? Or had I never been as good as I thought I once was?

"She's a Jap," he was saying. "A Jap. A whore Jap at that. Well hell, I guess they all are. But why would anybody be looking for her? What the fuck's wrong with you, fella?"

He still wasn't looking at me. Not really. He was mostly glancing over his shoulder at Miki, and buzzing all around, his eyes darting from surface to surface like a housefly.

In order to put me in the tub, he was forced to fold me up, placing my legs beneath me. With my arm tied straight down my body, my hand wasn't far from my ankle and the holster strapped to it. I was sure he would have removed the weapon, but realized how crazy it would be not to confirm.

"All you had to do was ask," he said. "I'd've let you fuck her."

Reaching down with my hand and shifting my weight so I could bring my leg back and up a bit, I felt my trouser for the holster and gun beneath. Neither were there.

Think. What can I do? How can I ...

It occurred to me that I might be able to push up with my legs and lunge toward him, but even if I could, which was doubtful from my folded, numb legs, I wouldn't be able to do more than bump into him. I couldn't even wrestle him for the knife, couldn't grab it even if I was able to knock it out of his hand.

I was a blunt object. Dead weight. Useless.

A young girl had lived a nightmare of rape and torture and imprisonment. I had had a chance to save her and failed. Hell, I couldn't even save myself.

There was nothing I could do, but I had to do something, had to try. Something.

Without a plan, without hope, without a prayer, I pushed myself up out of the tub just high enough to fall over the edge flat on the floor.

Paul's reaction was one of surprise then laughter.

In genuine amusement, he began laughing so hard I thought he might wet himself.

"What're you supposed to be? A log? You gonna roll over here and hurt me? Huh?"

Jerking back as far as I could, I kicked my bound legs as hard as I could at him, sweeping his legs out from underneath him.

He fell hard.

His back bent over the side of the tub as his head crashed into the other side, making a loud crack.

The knife fell to the floor and bounced toward me.

I reached for it, but couldn't get it, couldn't grasp the handle because my hand was bound too tight against my leg.

I leaned up to look at him.

He was not moving.

Had the blow to the head knocked him unconscious?

A few seconds later when he started moving, I realized he'd just had the wind knocked out of him.

I grasped for the knife again but it was no good.

I had no idea what to do, and I felt so weak and helpless.

Slinging myself around and rolling and pushing up as best I

could, I got to my feet, slamming into the door frame and bouncing back.

But somehow I managed to remain on my feet.

Having no other options, I jumped on top of him in the tub.

Jumping over and over again—and over again, I stomped him.

I stomped his chest and abdomen, his head and neck.

I jumped on him like a kid on a motel bed, only far more violently and far less fun.

I could hear bones cracking and fracturing, hear him moaning and groaning, crying and shrieking, but I didn't stop, just continued to stomp.

Eventually, exhausted and lightheaded, blood dripping from the stitches I had ripped loose in my abdomen, I lost my balance and collapsed on top of the kid.

Out of breath, out of my mind, for a long time I was unable to move.

Wheezing, coughing, panting, bleeding, I could feel my body coming down off the adrenaline high.

Soon I began to tremble, tremors running the length of my three limbs.

It took a while, but eventually I was able to get up again and work myself free.

Stumbling into the room and over to the bed, I could see that Miki was still breathing, was still alive. I staggered out of the room and into Ruth Ann's car with her.

Unsure exactly where the group was hiding, I went back to the area near the dunes where I had met with both Bunko and Rina. Parking on the side of the highway, I began blowing my horn and flashing my headlights.

Over and over again. Blowing. Flashing. Flashing. Blowing.

Inside of ten minutes, one of the young Japanese gunsels who worked for Miki's uncle appeared at my door, tapping on the glass with the butt of his revolver.

His eyes grew wide when he saw the condition Miki was in on the seat beside me.

"Get her mom and uncle now," I said. "Hurry."

He did.

Help arrived within minutes.

Bunko, Rina, and a handful of other young men and women whisked Miki away and I wondered if I'd ever see her again.

I then led her uncle and two carloads of young men back to the Magnolia and watched as they took Paul away to give him the big sendoff kill, if I hadn't already beaten them to it, then cleaned away all evidence and every trace that Miki, Rina, or I had ever been at the motel. They then torched the cabin where it had all happened—this after I talked them out of burning down the entire place.

Afterward, my head still filled with snakes, I drove back to Ruth Ann's, collapsed onto the couch, and fell fast asleep.

The nightmares came right away. And stayed.

29

"You're bleeding all over my sofa, soldier," Lauren said.

As I became less groggy and my vision improved, I could see the creature hovering over me was Ruth Ann looking like Lauren, and not Lauren herself.

"Sorry," I said. "I'm afraid it's in your car too. I'll clean everything—or have it done. I'm really sorry for all the trouble I've caused you."

"It's no trouble, fella. I keep telling you that. There's no one I'd rather have bleeding on my things than you."

I wasn't sure what to say, so I just smiled.

Following our conversation the night before I really thought she'd go back to her hair color and clothes. Why was she still in costume? If anything, she looked even more like Lauren today than she did then.

I was so tired, in so much pain. I was lonely and missing Lauren—missing her like a part of me had been removed. I glanced at where my right arm should be. Losing it, missing it, living without it was nothing compared to the loss of Lauren—the missing, the not living I was doing now.

I thought again about Ruth Ann's offer. God it would feel so good to lose myself in her, in the illusion of Lauren. Why couldn't I? Lauren would understand. Hell, she would want me to, so why couldn't I?

"Jimmy," Ruth Ann was saying.

"Yeah?"

"Where'd you go?"

"I'm here."

"You okay?"

"Yeah. Why?"

"The way you're looking at me ... like I'm ... You thought any more about what we talked about?"

I must have looked confused.

"About me ... us ... How I feel about you."

"I have."

"Have you reconsidered?"

"Why do you ask?"

"The way you were just looking at me."

"Oh. Sorry. I was just—"

"Don't be. I like it. Look some more. Look a lot."

"It's not that you're not ... It's not that I don't want ... I just can't."

"Okay. Sure. I get it. I just thought ... I'm telling you the way you were looking at me."

I was looking at her, thinking of her. It's always been her. It always will be.

"Anyway. I understand. I do. And I appreciate it. It's just ... if I were on the receiving end of that kind of ... Okay. Let's get you cleaned and stitched back up. And I'm not kidding—you've got to stop opening this wound back up."

"I'm not doing it by choice," I said. "You sure you're okay?"

"I'm fine. And I'll be even better soon. Promise. Don't worry about me, mister. And don't you go treating me any differently. I still want you here. Still want to help you. I mean it."

"Any luck getting the girls names or pictures?"

"It's not as easy as I thought it'd be. Need just a bit more time. I won't let you down. Promise."

After Ruth Ann had patched me up and I was cleaned and dressed and ready to begin again, I borrowed her phone to call Delton Rogers.

"Hiya, Jimmy," he said. "Any headway?"

"Not much, no. Unless you count Butch kidnapping and trying to kill me."

"Why would you count that?" he said.

"I didn't. Just thought you might want to."

"Okay. So let's count it. What's it mean?"

"Pretty sure it means he didn't have anything to do with whatever happened to Pete."

"Oh yeah? How da you figure?"

"He did it to try to find out what happened to him. Thought I had something to do with it. Planned on squaring it if I did."

"Could be a cover."

"I thought of that but Butch ain't that smart."

"Good point," he said. "What are you some kind of detective?"

"Not so you could tell," I said.

He laughed. "You're okay, Jimmy. I've always said so."

"Wouldn't be a bad idea to keep an eye on Butch."

"Always do," he said.

"And keep your other out for Cliff Walton."

"Yeah? Figured he was in Mexico or in a shallow grave or in a shallow grave in Mexico."

"Saw him downtown a few nights ago."

"Downtown? You take some chances, don't you?"

"He'll know where Howell and the others are. Pete too if he ever made it over there."

"Sure thing."

"I got a license plate off the car he was driving. Need you to run it for me."

"Give it'a me."

I did.

"I'll see what I can find out."

The moment I hung up the phone, it rang.

I started to answer it, but then realized what I was doing and stepped back to let Ruth Ann get it.

"Hello," she said, then paused. "Hold on."

She handed me the phone.

"Hello?"

"Hey ya, sugga," Mama Cora said. "How are you?"

"I'm okay, Mama. How are you?"

"Clipper tol' me how he saved you again. I got word to him the moment that fat cracker led you away from here. Tol' me later he's already followin' him for you at the time."

"Thank you."

"Oh," she said, her voice full of mirth, "you about to."

"I am?"

"Yes sir, safe money is you are."

"Why's that?"

"I got somethin' for you. Somethin' real good. Anarchist chap I know has a place in St. Andrews. Big old three-story house where they have meetings and events—political get-togethers, spiritual awakening encounters, art exhibits, meditation meet-ups. Shit like that."

"Yeah?"

"He's a queer fellow. Always thought he was harmless, but ... I'll pick you up in a quarter of an hour, dear."

"For what? Why? What's—"

"Didn't I say?"

"You did not."

"Because, darlin', they have a surrealist exhibit installed right now. And several of the pieces bear a remarkable resemblance to your dead girls."

30

"Most of these artists, most true surrealists," Adrian was saying, "see their work as an expression of the movement first and foremost. The medium, method—hell, the art itself, is secondary, an artifact of the philosophy."

Adrian Fromerson was a dainty, diminutive man, gaudy and gaunt. His bleach-blond hair was short and stood up in jagged clumps like a child who just woke up after having gone to bed with a wet head. His skin was pasty, but only showed on his face and hands. Every other inch of him was covered in a solid black suit and high-neck shirt that looked European. At just under five feet, he had the appearance of a boy playing dress-up.

He was dwarfed by the enormity of Mama Cora's three hundred plus pounds, which were wrapped in an orange and purple sari, her caramel skin glowing beneath a sheen of perspiration coming mostly from beneath her do-rag.

"Surrealism is a critique of Western culture, a response to its corruption," Adrian continued. "It's a fuck-you to conventional bourgeois bullshit. Whereas the Dadaist used protest, subversion, and straight out rebellion, surrealists are more subtle, more pragmatic. It's an intellectual revolution influenced by Freud and Marx."

Adrian's huge house was more a meeting hall and museum than a home, with books and brochures in the foyer, a lecture hall in the living room, crooks and crannies of couches and pillows like something out of Mama Cora's, and a surrealist art installation everywhere else.

From the outside, it appeared to be an old three-story Victorian, but inside it was both bohemian and radical, the center of a seditious, subversive revolution.

After a brief introduction and overview of his anarchist politics, he was now leading us through the creaky hardwood-floored house showing us the surrealism exhibit.

As best I could tell we were the only people here.

The works combined distorted images, odd perspectives, queer elements, and asymmetrical arrangements.

Human bodies, mostly women, had been deconstructed, disassembled, rearranged. Elongated humans had the heads of animals. Female torsos had dresser drawers opening from them. Men had erect penises for legs. Heads came out of navels. Shapes gave impressions of things far more than any semblance of actual depictions of the things themselves.

"See how the work involves elements of surprise, non sequiturs, and unusual and unexpected juxtapositions?" Adrian asked. "What you're seeing is liberation. As Guillaume Apollinaire said when he first coined the phrase, it reveals a truth beyond the real, a kind of surreal truth that transcends the obvious and actual. This is what revolution looks like."

One blobbish white woman in black thigh-high stockings had her breasts on her back so that they formed a kind of companion to her buttocks, the thin hint of a red nightgown showing between them, but she had no head.

Another featured a blue female form with shovels for legs

and penises for arms and the head of a hyena. She was walking through a forest of burning trees made mostly of men.

"Can you see? Do you know what this is? It's the unconscious on canvas, the depiction of dreams, the dissection of the dark corners of the human mind."

None of the work was as good as what I had seen in some of the books and magazines I'd read, but most weren't bad and a few were actually pretty good.

"What can you tell me about the artists involved in this show?"

"Most are European members of the movement that came here at the start of the war, but we've mixed in a few local and regional artists as well. I even have a piece or three. And Mama should, but I couldn't convince her."

"Nothin' I'm workin' on is quite finished yet, sugga," she said. "I'll have some work ready for the next one. Though … nothin' I have is as good as any of this."

"This is nothing. Wait 'til you see the work upstairs."

The paintings and sculptures on the second floor were far better than the first, their juxtapositions more startling, their disjointedness and disorientation more disconcerting. They were also more sexual and colorful and radical.

"Are you getting it?" he asked me. "Do you see now what is being done and why? In the same way Freud and other psychoan-alysts use hypnosis and other techniques to access the inner workings of the mind, surrealists unlock the depths of dreams and thoughts, bringing them up out of the underworld for us to witness. They express it so we can experience it. And it's exquisite, isn't it?"

I nodded. It really was. I was moved by them, mesmerized by their dreamlike quality, unsettled by their subversive and perver-sive power.

But nothing compared with the shock of the third floor—a single room known as Black and White Butchery that looked nearly identical to the crime scene photos of the four female victims.

The room was all black, including the floor. Faceless female mannequins painted white were posed on black silk drop cloths in various stages of disassemble and dissection. Several of the poses looked exactly like the manner in which the killer had arranged and displayed his dolls.

The walls were covered with paintings with strong resemblance to what was on the floor—except the white melting shapes representing the female form were even more dissected and distorted and they were joined by animal parts and other objects, all whitewashed, bright, overexposed, high contrast.

"Oh sweet Lord Jesus," Mama Cora said as we entered the room.

"What?" Adrian asked in shock. "What is it?"

"Just reminds me of something. That's all."

"I assure you this is as original as it gets. You won't see anything like it anywhere. Are you saying you have?"

"No, sugga. Nothin' like that."

"Then what?"

"Who's the artist?" I asked.

"Flaxon De Grasse. Why?"

"I need to talk to him."

"You think he the killer?" Mama asked. "Or just inspired him?"

"Killer?" Adrian asked in alarm. "What killer? What are you talking about? What's—"

He stopped abruptly as something caught his eye.

Turning, he walked over, stooped down, and picked up a small framed photograph from next to one of the mannequin displays.

"What the hell is—"

I walked over and looked over his shoulder at the picture. It was of the victim that most closely resembled the mannequin it was placed beside. Of much higher quality and artistic merit, the photograph looked like one from the crime scene set I had seen, but had to have been taken by the killer. I turned to look at the other displays. The other three that matched the victims also had small framed photos beside them.

"These weren't here before," Adrian said. "What is this? Are they real? They look real."

"You know the four girls mentioned in the paper?" Mama said.

"Really? Are you ... This is them? Oh my God. That means ... the killer has been in my home."

"Possibly several times," I said. "How do I get in touch with Flaxon?"

31

F laxon De Grasse lived at the end of a dock in a small shack on St. Andrew Bay. The dock was rickety, the gaps in its planks like missing piano keys, its pilings leaning at odd angles as if injured lovers pulling away from the source of their pain. All the slips were empty, the entire structure appearing abandoned.

It was early afternoon and the November day was bright but cold, the wind whipping off the bay bracing and occasionally biting.

In case De Grasse was the killer, Adrian, who tried to convince me there was no way he could be, had driven Cora home for me. Unable to locate Clip, I had phoned Delton Rogers to meet me. He was on his way—more for backup than anything else—but as I knocked on the sagging screen door I could tell it wouldn't be necessary. No one was home.

Nearly all of the windows and doors were open. Inside there was no movement, no presence, no sign anyone was there.

I walked down the dock to the next door, looking in the other windows as I did.

The cold breeze was damp and smelled of brine. Beneath the dock, the bay waters bobbed, the sounds of them slapping the pilings joining the cries and shrieks of birds and the distant clanging of riggings.

"Flaxon?" I called through the second screen door. "Anyone home?"

I waited a moment, then called out again—this time even louder.

After a few more moments, I eased the door open and slipped inside.

The small leaning room was dim and dank and obviously his workshop. Chains and hooks hanging from the ceiling and coming out of the walls held the dismembered parts of white mannequins. They dangled and rocked, their chains rattling with the shifting and creaking of the cabin.

His work area was dirty and disorganized, littered with trash and empty wine bottles—hundreds of empty wine bottles. Though old and well worn, his tools were in good shape and he had plenty of them. There was no question they could dismember a human body, but there was no evidence that they ever had.

The door connecting the workshop with the living area was open and I walked through it and into a room similar in size that held a cot, a small kitchen table with one chair, an old, scarred wardrobe, a rocking chair, and stacks of papers and books. Framed paintings leaned against the walls, none of it hung, all of it his work, and this room held even more trash and wine bottles. Like the workshop floor, the few spots of this one that were not actually covered were grime-streaked and paint-specked.

There was no bathroom or kitchen, and as far as I could tell, there was no electricity or plumbing. A couple of kerosene lanterns seemed the only sources of light when night fell.

I looked around a bit. In addition to art and philosophy books, most of the other literature seemed similar to what was in the foyer of Adrian's place.

From the workshop behind me, a small gray cat slunk into the room, part of a fish head in its mouth.

I looked around a little more but there was nothing else to see.

When I stepped out of the shack and began heading back down the dock, I could see Delt at the other end.

He wasn't alone.

Flanked by a detective I didn't recognize and two uniforms I did, he had come to arrest me.

As soon as they saw me, the two uniforms drew their guns.

Delt said something to them, then walked out to meet me alone as they lowered, but didn't holster, their weapons.

I walked slowly toward him. We met near the middle, far enough away from the others so they couldn't hear us.

"Delt," I said.

"Jimmy."

"Why now?" I asked. "You could've done this several times already."

"You dealt this play, partner."

"How's that?"

"Dispatcher recognized your voice. Told the captain."

I nodded.

"Left me no options."

"There are always options."

"Didn't see any," he said. "Sorry, pal."

Henry Folsom was a large man. Everything about him was thick. He was tall and middle-aged, but muscular—only some of which was beginning to turn to fat. He was a decent man, a tough and honest cop, and, at one time, he had been my boss.

"Jimmy," he said when he walked into the interview room.

"Captain."

"I don't know what's going on," he said. "That's what we're here to find out. But you know me. I'm fair. And at one time you were one of mine. In some ways I feel like you still are. You'll get a square deal from me and every break I can give you—and no matter what you did, I'll look out for you."

I nodded. "Thank you."

"I'm gonna be handling everything myself from this end, but because you used to work here, a detective from Tallahassee is going to conduct the interview and the investigation. You wanna attorney?"

I shook my head.

"You sure?"

"Yes, sir."

"Okay then. Let's get started."

He opened the door, and a trim man in a pressed shirt and spotless suit came in carrying a tablet of paper, a pencil, and a briefcase.

"This is Detective McDonald."

Balding with beady eyes behind small glasses, he looked more like an accountant than a cop.

"Call me Derris," he said.

After he placed his paper and pencil on the table and the briefcase carefully beside it, he extended his hand and I shook it.

"I've been told a lot about you," he said. "And I like what I've heard. You were a good cop, a hero. Some say you're a good detective and maybe you are. Maybe you're an innocent as I am. And maybe you're not. The point is, I'm only trying to find the truth. And at this moment I have no opinion about what that is. Understand? So tell me, what's the truth?"

"Before we get to any of that," I said, turning to Captain Folsom. "There's something you need to know. The place where I was when they picked me up ... the man who lives there has a connection to the killings—the four women that were dismembered."

"How do you even know they were—"

I cut him off and explained how I got involved and what led me to Flaxon. "I'm not saying he's the killer, just that there's a connection. May just be that his art is inspiring the killer. I don't know. But I wanted you to be able to follow up on it as soon as possible."

"I'll let our guys know."

He stepped out of the room, leaving the door ajar, and McDonald and I waited, remaining silent until he returned.

While he was away, I thought some more about how I could tell them what I needed to without revealing the part Lauren played. She was so integral, both to what happened and to me, my involvement, my ... everything—how could I ... She was the story. It began and ended with her.

"Okay," McDonald said. "Let's have it."

"The whole thing had to do with politics—the mayoral race. Frank Howell was behind it. He used a guy named Cliff Walton. Walt worked for the current mayor Harry Lewis, but was really there to spy, bully, and blackmail. He tried to kill me the night I left town with Lauren Lewis. I shot him in the leg and got away. I called Detective Mitchell and told him everything and where everyone involved was. They had all gathered at Howell's. He called his new partner Butch for backup. You can verify that. Butch got a call and was told to the report to the crime scene where the second of the four female victims was found. He was told Pete would be contacted and told the same thing, but Pete never showed. Later, when Butch went to Howell's, everyone was gone and there was no sign of Pete. He hasn't been seen since."

"You're saying you had nothing to do with the deaths of Freddy Moats, Margie Lehane, that little hood named Cab, your secretary, your partner—and the only one who can verify it is missing?"

"No. I'm saying—"

"You've said enough," Harry Lewis said.

I looked up to see him standing in the doorway.

"This man was working for me and my wife when the crimes you're asking him about were committed. Not only were the victims brutally beaten in a manner impossible for a one-armed man—a left arm at that—but he was with me during the time of each murder. I'll swear to it in court. He has acted nobly and honorably and does not deserve to be treated like anything other than the hero he is. Now, he's leaving with me. Or you can try to arrest us both and see how that works out for you."

32

"Thanks," I said.

Harry and I were standing out in front of the station. It was late afternoon, the sun starting its final drastic descent, the temperature dropping, shop lights, streetlights, and headlights more pronounced now. The heavy traffic on Harrison moved slowly. Horns honked. Breaks squealed. Gears grinded.

"Let me tell you something, fella," Harry said. "I realize how much I owe you. And not just for helping me realize my lifelong dream to serve the public, but ... well, Lauren left me a letter. The priest who was killed brought it to me. I know what you meant to her, what all you did for her."

"But—"

"Look. You don't have to say anything. I'm not foolish. I know the nature of your relationship. You're okay. She was more like a daughter to me than anything else."

I nodded, not sure what to say.

The sidewalks were crowded. People everywhere. Wainwright shipyard employees cashing their checks. Servicemen socializing with girls. Men in trousers and shirt sleeves. Women in dresses. Babies in strollers. Kids trailing behind parents. In and out of shops, restaurants, motels. On the balcony of the Tennessee House, coming and going from the Ritz theater, every other person in some type of uniform—army, navy, marines, and outnumbering them all, air force and Red Cross nurses.

"Now," he said. "I don't think you'll have any more problems with the police. So let's find those responsible for her death and make things right. Starting with Frank Howell. I know others were involved, but it begins and ends with him."

"It does and I will start with him or end with him, but I saw Cliff Walton and I have a lead on him."

"Really? Good. Double-crossin' bastard."

For all the power Harry had, for all the influence he wielded, he looked old and feeble. His drooping skin was whiskey-reddened, broken blood vessels webbed the puffy area around his nose, and the blackish bags beneath his blue eyes were enormous.

He reached into his pocket and handed me a set of keys and a hundred dollar bill, then another to keep the first from getting lonely.

"This'll help with expenses," he said.

"It certainly will."

"And don't spare any. There's plenty more where those came from. And the keys are to that Ford over there. It's yours. Just find these people and punish them as quickly as possible. Understood?"

I nodded that it was.

When Harry had gone, I went back in and found Henry Folsom in his office.

"Be careful Jimmy," he said.

"Always am."

His eyes drifted over to the spot where my right arm should be.

"Well, almost always."

He was taken aback a bit, and I could tell that him looking at my stump had been unconscious, involuntary.

"Sorry."

"Everything I said in there was true," I said. "Just wanted you to know."

"I never doubted it was, but two things. One, you left a lot out. And two, there's a way to do things and this ain't it."

"That's why I'm here. I had nothing to do with what the mayor just did. I'm telling the truth. Frank Howell was behind everything. He used Ann Everett, Payton Rainer, and the guy I mentioned to you—Cliff Walton. And another thing, the others may have blown town, but Walt didn't. I saw him just a couple of streets over from here a few nights ago. Keep an eye out for him. He walks with a limp now."

"Don't we all."

I thought about just how true that statement was.

"Any word on De Grasse?"

"Who?"

"The artist connected to the killings."

"That's his name?"

"Yeah."

"No."

We were quiet a minute.

"Who killed Ray?" he asked.

I turned around and closed the door.

Before I spoke, I started to say something about this being off the record, but knew there was no such thing for a cop— particularly one like Folsom.

"I did."

"You better sit down."

I did.

"Let's have it," he said.

I gave it to him.

"He killed July, our secretary. She stumbled upon records that showed he was secretly following someone he was obsessed with."

"A woman?"

"Of course."

"The Lewis dame?"

"He said he didn't mean to kill July and I half believed him. And that's not why I shot him. It was in self-defense. This gut shot I got—" I indicated my abdomen, "—he did that. It's what I got treated for in Tallahassee. You can verify it. I was trying to get to Lauren—Mrs. Lewis—to get her some help. Had to shoot Ray to do it. He stood in the way. He fired first. It's a clean shoot, Captain."

When I had mentioned getting treated in Tallahassee, something flared in a dark corner of my mind. What was it? What was it about Tallahassee or treatment or ... There was something there, but I just couldn't get at it.

He thought about what I had said for a long moment. "I appreciate you coming back and telling me, Jimmy. I do. You're okay."

"I wanna find Pete," I said. "You have any idea where he is or what happened to him?"

He shook his head. "Hell, son, I knew a lot less before you told me what you did tonight."

"Can you get my medical records?" I asked.

"I'm a nurse, fella," Ruth Ann said. "Whatta you think?"

I was at a pay phone on Harrison. I had started to borrow a phone inside the station, but didn't want anyone to overhear our conversation.

"Would you?" I asked.

"Already did."

"You did?"

"You thought I've been taking care of you blind, fella? Say, whatta ya think I am, brainless?"

"You got the ones from Tallahassee?"

"I got 'em all. All I could find that is. I'm a very thorough girl. Why?"

"I need to see them."

"They're right here. You can see 'em when you get home."

Her use of the word home wasn't lost on me. I had unwittingly been playing house with her. And I had to stop. I cared very deeply for her, owed her so much, but it was no good. I wasn't in love with her, and I could never be. I had my one great love and had fucked it up forever. Didn't matter how much Ruth Ann dressed or talked or looked like Lauren. She wasn't Lauren. And could never be.

As I hung up the phone, a car pulled up to the curb. It was Miki Matsumoto's uncle.

He motioned for me to get in. I did.

"Good evening, Mr. Rirey."

"Evening."

The driver pulled away from the curb and continued down Harrison very slowly in the fray.

"I ah wisha to thank you for the ah safe return ofa my niece."

"How is she?"

"Improving. It willa take ah rong time fora minda to ah heal, but she is strong. Will be okay."

I nodded. "That's good."

"Ita concern me thata youa spending so mucha time ata porice station."

"It's unrelated," I said. "I'll never say anything to anyone. No matter what. You have my word."

"Whya they reta you goa?"

"The mayor made them."

"We ah will be watching youa very crosrey. Ifa we evena think youa going to talk, we willa be forced ah to takah you outa."

At that, the driver pulled over to the curb and I got out.

We had driven several blocks down Harrison, so I started

walking back in the opposite direction toward the new Ford Harry had provided for me.

The sun was down and the temperature had fallen, a cold breeze blowing between the buildings, winding around the traffic and through the pedestrians.

I had no overcoat on, only an insufficient suit coat. I gathered it around me, hunched into the wind, head down, dodging the stream of sidewalkers.

I had walked less than two blocks when Clip pulled up in a no doubt stolen black Packard.

"Nice night for a walk," he said through the open passenger window.

"Bracing."

"I'd offer you a ride, but somebody might think I your butler."

I smiled and got in the car. "That true if you don't offer but I get in anyway?"

"No. Then you just a white man doin' what white men do."

"Which is?"

"Whatever the hell they wants."

"You been on Butch?"

He nodded. "Was when I saw you get in the car with the Jap. He had just come back to the station. Broke off him to see if you's 'bout to get your ass shot again."

"He was thanking me for my help getting his niece back."

"Thanking you? Didn't look like no kind of thank you I ever seen. Why'd he drop your ass off where he did if he was all grateful and shit?"

"Anything on Butch?"

"He ain't okay and he don't do much police work. Hell, he don't do much of nothin', but I ain't caught him doin' much of anything too illegal either."

I thought about it.

"He a bully and he ain't none too bright, but he ain't into too much. Not sayin' he not dangerous. He's bent, that's for sure, but he mostly bumblin'."

"Bumbling?" I asked, shooting him a look.

He nodded and smiled.

We were quiet a moment, his car still idling at the curb.

"You gonna give me a ride back to my car?" I asked.

"What? I your butler now?"

"Just wondered why we still sitting here."

"We talkin'. Enjoying the sights and sounds of Harrison in the warmth of my au-to-mo-bile as we confer about a case."

"Oh."

"'Sides, you ain't gonna be wantin' to go back to your car after you aks me about that other big bitch."

"Walt?" I said. "You seen him."

"I have."

"And?"

"And he close by."

"How close?"

"The trunk."

33

"How's the leg?" I asked.

"Improving," Walt said. "Which is more than can be said for your arm."

We were in a small clearing in the woods near Bayou George we had used before for this same thing.

We had Walt sitting on the base of a tree stump, his legs tied to it, his upper body tied to the tree behind it. Both had splatters of dried blood on them from our previous visits to the woods.

Above us, the starless sky was dark. Around us, the deep woods were even darker, the headlights from the idling Packard some fifteen feet behind us the only illumination in the area.

Beyond the clearing in every direction for miles and miles there was only the dense dark forest.

Unlike previous visits, the woods were eerily quiet. The only sounds besides those we were making were the whisper of a thin wind snaking through the trees and the hum of the engine.

"I'm not going to make a lot of threats," I said.

"Good. 'Cause I wouldn't believe them anyway. 'Sides, I—"

Clip stepped forward and punched him in the face, breaking

his nose and banging his head back into the trunk of the tree behind him.

"Now the time for you to be listenin'," he said.

Our bodies were blocking most of the light from reaching Walt and I wondered how Clip was able to tag him so well with the use of only one eye.

"Why exactly wouldn't you believe my threats?"

He laughed. "You're a lover, not a fighter."

I smiled as I thought about it.

"You shot me in the leg, sure," he said. "So yeah, you're a leg shooter. Ain't sayin' you ain't tough and can't dish out some pain and punishment, just that you won't kill a man in cold blood."

"You think that true of me too?" Clip asked.

"I don't, actually, but it applies to you 'cause you workin' for him."

"Like I was saying, I'm not going to make a lot of threats," I said again. "You know how this works. Answer my questions honestly and this'll go a hell of a lot easier for you."

"Ask whatever you like," he said. "I ain't singin'."

"What happened after I left Howell's the night I shot you in the leg?"

He didn't say anything.

Clip went to work on him—first his body, then his head, then back to his body—giving him one hell of a beating.

"What happened after I left?" I asked.

He turned and spit, a long string of blood trailing after it. He then shook his head. "Tol' ya. I don't sing."

I remembered how much he sang after I shot him at Howell's that night.

"Why didn't you leave town?"

"Work to do. 'Sides, this is my town."

"Pretty sure the town don't know that," Clip said.

"Did the others?"

He didn't respond.

"Did the others leave town?" I said.

I reached inside my coat beneath what was left of my right arm and withdrew my revolver.

He seemed not to notice.

Placing the barrel near the spot where the other round had gone in, I squeezed the trigger.

He let out a shriek and a long string of threats and profanity.

"What happened that night?" I said. "Where is everybody?"

"Leg shooter," he said. "All you'll ever be."

I smiled. Then shot him in the arm.

Clip laughed.

Walt let out more shrieks, more cries, more curses, more threats.

"So there's nothing I can do to convince you to talk?" I asked. "Handing you over to Henry Folsom is my only play?"

"You give me to the cops and everyone—and I do mean everyone—will know what a filthy whore that slut was."

His words set off something inside me so feral I didn't recognize it—mostly by reminding me Lauren was dead in large part due to him.

Awkwardly thumbing back the hammer with my anger and adrenaline-jittery left hand, I stepped forward and pressed the barrel of the gun into the crease just above his eyes.

"If you don't think I'll put your lights out after what you did to her, you greatly mistake me. Now, you answer my goddamn questions right now or I will fuckin' flip your switch off permanently. And if you ever say anything about her again, it will be the last thing you ever say. I swear it."

He didn't respond, but there seemed to be something different in his demeanor.

"Now, tell me what the fuck happened after I left."

"We left too. Right after you."

"Where are the others now?"

"In the shallow graves where I put them."

"Pete too?"

"Who?"

"Pete Mitchell. Cop. My old partner."

"Nothing to do with him. Why would you think I—"

"He went over there that night to arrest y'all."

"Well he got there too late I guess. Never saw him."

"Why kill your boss and coconspirators?"

"You have no idea what's really going on," he said.

"Enlighten me."

"Some detective," he said, then nodding at Clip, "The one-eyed jig can see better than you."

"Where'd you bury them?"

He started laughing. "I put them in the whore's grave."

I hit him hard across the face, the gun in my hand tearing into his flesh, leaving a flap of skin dangling from his cheek.

"Where are they buried?"

"What're you gonna do, shoot my other arm and leg?"

"Yes," I said, and did.

It took a while for him to regain composure, and even then he was breathing heavily, crying, and wincing in pain.

"Goddamn I'm gonna enjoy all that happens to you," he said.

"Happens to me?"

"You have no idea the pain and misery in store for you. One hell of a goddamn storm of it's gonna rain down on your head."

I thought about all I had been through and how nothing that had ever happened or could ever happen could compare to losing Lauren.

"You haven't begun to suffer," he said.

"Where did you bury them?"

He shook his head.

Clip moved in front of him and placed the barrel of his revolver in Walt's crotch.

"One chance to save your little dick," Clip said. "Only one.

Think long and hard before you answer. You only gets one chance."

"Where did you bury them?"

When he hesitated, Clip jammed the gun down even harder and pulled back the hammer.

"Okay. Okay. It's actually not far from here. Little further up on 231. Close to a lake. I can show you."

34

And ten minutes later, he did.

He was in shock from the trauma he had suffered and weak from the loss of blood, but he managed to take us to the spot, continuing to act defiant and undefeated all the way.

I had noticed a shovel in the trunk of the Packard when we had pulled Walt out the first time, and wondered why it was there. Clip had to know I wasn't going to kill Walt and bury him in the woods.

As he opened the trunk and removed it, I asked, "Why'd you bring that?"

"Didn't. This his car," he said, nodding toward Walt as he stumbled toward the huge oak they were buried beneath. "Hell, this probably the shovel he used to bury them with."

We followed Walt over to the spot, walking slowly as he hobbled along in front of us.

"Soon as I show you, I want a goddamn doctor."

He led us to a patch of dirt not far from the tree, then collapsed onto the ground.

Clip started digging.

"I doin' this 'cause your ass got one arm and you can't dig for shit, not 'cause I your butler."

"Nobody would ever think otherwise."

It didn't take him long to hit something solid, and in a while the upper half of three bodies were mostly exposed.

Serious decay had started and much of their skin was already missing, but there was enough to tell they were the bodies of Frank Howell, Payton Rainer, and Ann Everett.

"Still don't see why you killed them," I said.

"You don't see anything. That's what I keep telling you. Doesn't matter. You'll be dead soon. Then you'll have plenty of time to work it out in hell."

"If that's true, what's the harm in telling me what I'm not seeing?"

"I ain't sayin' shit else. Now get me to a goddamn doctor."

"What are we gonna do with him?" Clip asked.

"Can't turn him in," I said. "Can't have him telling them about Lauren."

"Only leave one option."

"I know."

"I'll do it," he said, starting to withdraw his weapon.

I shook my head. "No. My decision. I've got to be the one to do it."

He looked at me for a long moment, his eye studying me intently. "You sure?"

I nodded slowly. "He killed her."

I had been thinking about this since the moment he had threatened to do damage to Lauren, and no matter which way I turned it, which way I approached it, it all came back to the same thing. Cliff Walton couldn't be allowed to live. And it wasn't just because of what he'd reveal to everyone about Lauren now, but that he was a big part of the reason she was dead. I couldn't turn him in. I couldn't let him go. That left only one thing to do, but could I do it?

I had killed before—not many times, but enough that I knew what it was like, the toll it took, the cost it exacted, the residual effects in the mind, the karmic ripples on the soul. But I had never executed a man before, never killed in cold blood. Could I do it? And having done it, could I live with it? The former was the real question because the latter was made moot by the fact that I wouldn't have to live with it long.

"Use his gun," Clip said, handing it to me. "Then we wipe it down and drop it in the hole with him and the others."

As I took the gun I thought I should have Clip shoot me and put me in the same hole. After all, I was as guilty as the rest of them, just as responsible for Lauren's death—more so, actually. If I weren't a dead man walking, I would—or hoped I would. Maybe I'd live long enough to find out what happened to Pete and who's killing the young girls and to find out if there's anything to what Walt's been saying, but couldn't imagine it'd be much longer than that.

I walked over to Walt.

He was slumped over as if already dead, his bloody arms and legs dangling limply, his blood and sweat-soaked hair glistening in the headlights from his car.

"Did you kill the priest?" I asked.

He looked up slowly, his weak eyes barely open.

"Not intentionally. Was aiming for you."

"I'm going to kill you now and toss your body in the same hole with your coconspirators and victims."

He tried to laugh, but nothing much came out. "No you're not, Mr. leg shooter ... and arm ... Mr. leg and arm shooter."

There was a slight slur to his words, and it was taking him a long time to get them out.

"I'm not doing it because you killed the priest or those twisted bastards in the hole. I'm going to punch your ticket for what you did to Lauren. That's it. Understand?"

"Go fuck yourself."

He was growing more pathetic by the moment.

Clip appeared beside me. "He be dead soon. Just wait a while and you won't have to do it."

"But I do. I have to do it."

He nodded.

Stepping forward and thumbing back the hammer of his own weapon, I placed it between his eyes.

"Let me live and I'll tell you what's coming, what's going to happen to you. And I won't tell anyone about the … ah, Mrs. Lewis. I swear it."

"You wanna say a prayer, now's the time."

He shook his head.

"Anything else you want to say to us?"

"Just how goddamn glad I am you're gonna get what's comin' to you."

I started to pull the trigger, but couldn't.

"Let me live. Get a doctor to patch me up. I'll tell you everything. I know things you need to know. I'll tell you what really happened to her."

"Who?"

"You know who. Don't shoot me. Get me some help and I'll tell you."

"Last chance. Tell me now."

"You're not gonna do it. You can't."

He was right. I tried again, and just couldn't do it. I squeezed the trigger, but only to a point, then released it again.

Snippets of Lauren's letter came then. Unbidden, but never unwelcome.

Our love, mine for you and yours for me, has forever changed me. And though it is us, from us, a part of us, it also is beyond us. Through you I've experienced a love that I can only describe as divine.

Please know how very deeply I love you. Please don't ever stop loving me that same way.

We'll have eternity.

All my love, all of me,

Your Lauren

I thought about how much Lauren wouldn't want me to do this, how she would plead with me for my sake, not his, but then I pictured her in the ground, her precious flesh that used to press against mine, that smooth, sweet-smelling skin that I kissed and caressed so often, now rotting off her like that of her disfigured killers in the opening in the earth behind me, and I squeezed the trigger, the loud rapport echoing through the quiet woods and through the emptiness in the center of my soul.

35

I t was Thanksgiving.

I wasn't thankful. I was depressed.

I had had too much to drink the night before when I had come in from killing Walt. Actually, there was something to be thankful for. I was thankful that Frank Howell, Payton Rainer, Ann Everett, and Cliff Walton were dead.

I was hung over and hungry.

But mostly I was numb. I felt little of anything except a certain satisfaction at having put Walt in the ground.

In those moments when I wasn't completely numb, I felt lonely. I was as alone and isolated as I had ever been—and that was saying something.

I missed Lauren. I always missed Lauren. Her absence was both a constant dull ache and a continuous sharp pain. But I also missed July and even Ray and Ruth Ann, my old drinking pal. As it was, she wasn't Lauren and she wasn't herself, and I don't think she realized just how much I missed her, how what she was doing left me with no one.

The president had made a proclamation for Thanksgiving back on the eleventh that the paper reran today.

Proclamation 2600 - Thanksgiving Day, 1943

November 11, 1943

By the President of the United States of America

A Proclamation

God's help to us has been great in this year of march toward world-wide liberty. In brotherhood with warriors of other United Nations our gallant men have won victories, have freed our homes from fear, have made tyranny tremble, and have laid the foundation for freedom of life in a world which will be free.

Our forges and hearths and mills have wrought well; and our weapons have not failed. Our farmers, victory gardeners, and crop volunteers have gathered and stored a heavy harvest in the barns and bins and cellars. Our total food production for the year is the greatest in the annals of our country.

For all these things we are devoutly thankful, knowing also that so great mercies exact from us the greatest measure of sacrifice and service.

Now, therefore, I, Franklin D. Roosevelt, President of the United States of America, do hereby designate Thursday, November 25, 1943, as a day for expressing our thanks to God for His blessings. November having been set aside as "Food Fights for Freedom" month, it is fitting that Thanksgiving Day be made the culmination of the observance of the month by a high resolve on the part of all to produce and save food and to "share and play square" with food.

May we on Thanksgiving Day and on every day express our gratitude and zealously devote ourselves to our duties as individuals and as a nation. May each of us dedicate his utmost efforts to speeding the victory which will bring new opportunities for peace and brotherhood among men.

In Witness Whereof, I have hereunto set my hand and caused the seal of the United States of America to be affixed.

DONE at the City of Washington this 11th day of November, in the year of our Lord nineteen hundred and forty-three, and of the Independence of the United States of America the one hundred and sixty-eighth.

FRANKLIN D. ROOSEVELT

"You okay?" Ruth Ann asked.

I nodded, but knew there was no way it was convincing.

"What is it?"

I had just finished showering and dressing, and was about to take some aspirin and head back out to De Grasse's place.

I was moving very slowly.

"What is it?" she asked again.

"Rough day," I said.

"Oh yeah? How long's it been since you had one that wasn't?"

"Been a while."

She pulled out one of the chairs from the small dining table.

"Sit down. Let me feed you and get you fixed up," she said. "Don't have much of a traditional meal, but I have—"

"I'm fine. I've got to get back over to—"

"Sit down," she said. "I'll be quick."

I sat down.

She brought in a bowl of warm water, a washcloth, and her medical kit and set them on the table beside me.

"Just relax," she said.

She still looked like Lauren—all but the eyes—and her ministrations moved me deeply. After all the hardness and horror and violence and death of the past few days, her tender touch was nearly too much, and I could feel myself melting into it.

Unbuttoning my shirt, she pulled up my undershirt and examined my wounds.

"Take a deep breath and let it out slowly," she said. "Now another. Just relax. Let everything go. Breathe out all the badness. Breathe in love and peace and goodness. That's it." She paused. "Why'd you want your medical records?" she asked.

"Huh?"

"Sorry. We can talk about it later."

"No. Now is good. What did they treat me for in Tallahassee?"

"Gunshot. Why?"

"That's all?"

"Yeah. Why?"

"Why am I not sick?"

"Whatta you mean?"

"I should be sicker. I'm dying, right? Why am I not—"

"Of what? No you're not dying. Oh. I see. You thought she gave you—"

"I gave it to her."

The night I had left town with Lauren, I had discovered that she was dying, that Howell and Rainer and Everett and Walt were blackmailing her into getting Harry to drop out of the race.

I could still remember every second of the moment I discovered the truth.

I had broken into Ann Everett's house on Cherry Street and found a large envelope in a hidden compartment in the base of an ornate grandfather clock.

My heart had started racing as I opened it.

Lauren's medical records and detailed notes were inside.

The first word the beam of my flashlight had fallen on was a dirty word, the kind that led to blackmail, ended political aspirations, and took lives. Few words were as powerful or as deadly.

It explained Lauren's behavior, her episodes, everything.

Lauren had a disease with virtually no early sign of infection. She had a small, non-painful nodule or lesion, which she had ignored. It had gone away in just a few weeks. But untreated, her disease had progressed to the next stage.

As her lesion was going away, she got a reddish-brown rash on the palms of her hands and the soles of her feet. For a while, she had a fever, swollen glands, a sore throat, weight loss, headaches, and fatigue. Again, it was left untreated, and again, it progressed. As her rash began to disappear, the infection was still in her body, but there were very few symptoms and no outward signs of the disease, and all the while it was damaging her brain, heart, liver, eyes, bones, and joints.

Lauren had put off going to the doctor for as long as she could —perhaps because of how busy she was with the campaign or maybe because she suspected what it was. When she couldn't delay any longer, she trusted Ann Everett's recommendation of Payton Rainer, who administered a blood test called the Wasserman. But instead of treating her with the arsenic preparation and sulfa-like drug known as Salvarsan 606, he began to blackmail her—not for money, but to remove her husband from the mayoral race.

And Lauren couldn't go anywhere else for treatment.

She had syphilis.

I thought Margie had given it to me and I had given it to her. I truly thought there could be no other explanation. It's what made me even more guilty than Walt and Rainer and the rest.

"No, you didn't," Ruth Ann was saying. "After I saw her records, I was concerned she may have given it to you, but I gave you the Wasserman. You're clean."

"I'm ... what? What are you saying? It can't be ... I can't be—"

"You are. All this time you thought you gave it to her? You poor man."

I sat there in stunned silence, more in shock than Walt had been after having been shot in his legs and arms.

That thought brought back the pathetic image of Walt slumped on the ground, blood oozing from the gash in his face and through the holes in his clothes.

"You're sure?" I asked.

"Absolutely positive."

"So Margie didn't have it," I said, still reeling, trying to understand, my mind searching for something to moor to.

"Guess not. Or if she did, she didn't give it to you."

I thought about that, feeling guilty for all the hateful, horrible things I had thought about Margie.

"Is it sinking in, soldier?" she asked. "You didn't give it to her."

"It's starting to," I said. "But if I didn't, then who the hell did?"

36

"Sorry again, Jimmy," Delton Rogers said when Clip and I walked up. "Didn't know what else to do. Glad it worked out for you. Knew Folsom would be fair. Oh, and happy Thanksgiving."

He was leaning on his car not far from the dock, smoking conspicuously, easy for De Grasse to spot, particularly if he were suspicious and operating in a heightened state of paranoia.

"No sign of De Grasse?"

"No."

He ignored Clip and Clip ignored him right back.

"We've searched the place. Some creepy shit in there, but no sign of crime. No evidence of murder."

The bay was dark and quiet, the only sounds the gentle slap of the water against the pilings and the occasional foghorn in the distance.

The breeze blowing in off the bay was cold and constant and caused my eyes to tear. Clip and I were both in overcoats and hats, and were warm enough except for our faces.

All the streetlamps in the area were off because of the blackout, causing the ember of Delt's smoke to glow even brighter in the dark night. Clip and I lit up a couple of Old Golds, our embers joining his in the gloom.

"Found out anything else about him?" I asked.

"Got no record here. Don't know about where he came from. Hell, they may've sent him here 'cause he likes cutting up girls."

"Could be."

"Captain told us to keep our eyes out for that Cliff Walton fella. You seen him again?"

I swallowed hard.

"Y'all lookin' for him," Clip said, "just a matter of time 'fore he be in custody. Bet he can feel the net of justice drawing in on him right now. 'Course he probably blew town already."

"Did if he knew Delt was after him," I said.

We were quiet a moment, the sounds of the dark, lonely bay the only ones filling our ears, and I thought again of what Ruth Ann had told me. Had I really not killed Lauren? Had I really not given her the disease that had cut her life so short? And if I hadn't, who had? Who else was she seeing or had she seen? Why hadn't she told me? Had she been raped or had she been unfaithful? I had to find out. I wished I could talk to Father Keller. He'd know. Knew.

The silence was broken by Delt's radio squawking through the partially open window of his car. He opened the door, sat down, grabbed the mic, and responded to the dispatcher, who informed him that another body had been found and told him to report to the crime scene.

I recognized the address she gave him. It was the anarchist art gallery of Adrian Fromerson.

I pulled the car up in front of Adrian's old three-story Victorian house and parked behind Delt. Since we had been so close, we were the first to arrive. Avoiding cops as often as he could, Clip had remained behind to keep an eye out for De Grasse.

The front door was open, the dainty, diminutive figure of

Adrian Fromerson partially filling it, his short, jagged bleach-blond hair backlit by the chandelier in the foyer behind him.

"The hell is that?" Delt asked me.

"That's your host," I said.

"Oh God. What are we walking into?"

I looked forward to Delt's and the other cops' reaction to both Adrian and his art show.

"Jimmy, can you believe it?" Adrian said as we stepped up onto the porch. "It's just so ... to think the killer was here ... again ... in my house. That he actually installed one of his exhibits in my ..."

"Have you touched anything?" Delt asked.

"No, sir."

"Is anyone else here?"

"Just me."

"Have you searched the entire house?"

"Well, no. I haven't."

"Let's start with that. Jimmy, you help?"

I nodded.

We withdrew our weapons and began a systematic search of the huge house.

Delt and I split up, so I didn't get to see much, but any chance I got I watched him react to the distorted images, odd perspectives, queer elements, and asymmetrical arrangements of the deconstructed, disassembled, and rearranged female forms.

Mostly he just shook his head as the expressions on his face ranged from revulsion to incomprehension.

After searching every floor but the third, we collected Adrian from the front porch and went to look at the crime scene, sirens in the distance announcing the soon arrival of the others.

The single room of the third floor was exactly as it had been when I was here before—all black, faceless female mannequins painted white posed on black silk drop cloths in various stages of disassemble and dissection—only now in the center of it all was a new murder victim displayed in such a way as to be nearly indistinguishable from the rest of the exhibit.

Like the other victims before her, this latest one had been dissected and dismembered, drained of all blood, cleaned, her pale white body displayed on a black silk cloth. Like the other victims, her upper and lower body had been bisected, her arms and legs cut off. Unlike them, her hands and feet had also been severed. She was splayed spread-eagle, her arms and legs swapped. Every part of her had roughly six inches in between it and the part closest to it. Instead of her arms extending out to her hands, her legs did in their place. Instead of her legs extending down to her feet, her arms did. But as shocking as all of this was, nothing could match the visceral jolt of what was above her shoulders. Sawn off at the neck, her head had been removed and was missing. In its place, the bleached bright white skull of a cow, complete with long, sharp horns.

"Fuck me," Delt said. "I mean, goddamn. I just mean ... hell, I saw the others, but this ... this is just ..."

"I know."

"This is all the work of that De Grasse fella?" Delt asked.

"It is," Adrian said. "All but the ... but that."

"What the hell are we dealing with?"

"An artist," Adrian said.

"So it's got to be De Grasse, right?"

"Seems likely," I said. "But he could just be inspiring him. What else can you tell us about him?" I asked Adrian.

"He's—"

"What the fuck?" Butch said as he entered. "Is that real?"

"It is," Delt said.

Butch glanced over at us.

"The hell they doing here, Delt?"

"Adrian owns the place and Jimmy came with me from—"

"No civilians."

"But Butch, we—"

"No exceptions."

I turned and started out, Adrian following me.

"Nothing personal, pal," Butch said. "I mean that."

After leaving Adrian's, I drove back to check on Clip at De Grasse's place. Unlike Delt, Clip was not visible—neither he nor his car could be seen.

I pulled in and drove down away from the entrance to the dock and parked and waited. In a few minutes, Clip opened the passenger door and got in.

"Anything?" I asked.

"Not a thing."

"If he's the killer and he's letting us know by displaying the most recent body in his art exhibit, don't imagine he'll ever come back here."

"And if he do, and he not the killer, what good is he to us?"

I nodded slowly as I thought about it. "He might know something."

"Might."

"You up for keeping an eye on the place a little longer?"

"Sho. This a motherfucker I like to meet."

"Whatta I owe you so far?"

"More than you got," he said.

"How much?"

"Five dollars."

I pulled out one of Harry Lewis's crisp new hundreds and handed it to him.

He lit up, unable to help himself from grinning.

"Goddamn."

"I know."

"Hope you ain't thinkin' I can break this bitch for you."

I laughed. "It's all yours."

"Son of a bitch but you know how to put money in a nigga's pocket."

37

Cliff Walton haunted my dreams.

In the first one, I couldn't kill him. No matter what I did, he wouldn't die. I shot him over and over again—in the arms and legs and chest and head—and he just kept talking about all the horrible things he would say about Lauren as soon as he could get to the police or paper. Abandoning the gun, I stabbed him repeatedly with a pocket knife—hacking and chopping and spearing until we were both blood-covered and coughing, and all he did was kept talking, kept telling me all the ways in which he was going to torture me as soon as he got free. Eventually, I got the shovel and went to work on him, but even that was no good.

In the second dream, Walt was dead, but I couldn't burry him.

No matter what I tried, I just couldn't seem to get the hole dug and the body in it. Even with both my arms, which I had in the dream, I couldn't get the dirt to stay out of the hole. Every shovel I threw out would reappear back in immediately. Then, when I did finally have a small hole dug, I couldn't pull his body into it. I tried everything, but something was holding him back, and nothing I did could free him. The sun was coming up and I could hear cops approaching, but I couldn't get him buried. They were going to discover what I had done. They were going to lock me up. I was going to jail, maybe even be put to death, and I was powerless to prevent it no matter how feverishly I dug.

Waking, heart pounding, gasping for breath, and drenched in sweat, I shoved myself up unsteadily from the couch and stumbled to the kitchen sink and stuck my head under the tap.

Back in the rack, it took me a while to fall asleep again, but when I did, I dreamt of Lauren.

At first, I was trying to get to her, but couldn't. Harry was keeping me away. Everywhere I went to meet her, he'd arrive before me and whisk her away. Other times he'd have Walt do it.

Then we were together, making love in my bed at the Cove, but just as I was about to come, Harry banged on the door, saying he knew Lauren was in there with me, demanding for her to come out so he could take her home.

Suddenly, we were at Margie's, borrowing her bed, and this time Margie, Harry, and Walt were trying to get in—knocking on the door, tapping on the windows, calling to us.

It felt so good to be inside her—truly the best feeling in the world—and yet I couldn't completely enjoy it because the others were right outside, making so much noise, trying to get in.

"Ignore them," she whispered in my ear.

"I can't."

"Concentrate. I want you to finish before they come in and take me away from you."

"Is that what they're going to do?"

"I'm afraid so, darling."

"But—"

"Don't think of that now. I want you to finish first. Let me help you."

She slid down between my legs and took me in her mouth. God, it felt so good, so soft and warm, her skilled movements so tense yet tender. But it was no good. I couldn't come—and not just because of the distracting noise and the possibility they could burst in at any moment, but knowing they were going to take her away from me.

I was so hard and wanted to come so bad, but I couldn't and I was growing more frustrated by the moment.

I awoke a little while later to discover I really was in Lauren's mouth and that no one was trying to break in.

Relaxing into it, I grabbed the top of her head with my hand and began to thrust up into her open, hungry mouth.

I couldn't recall being this hard, this turned on, in a very, very long time. It had been so long, in fact, since I had been intimate, been sexual at all, and it felt so damn good, I was sure I wouldn't be able to last much longer before I exploded into her mouth.

But just as I was about to, she stopped.

"I want you inside me," Ruth Ann said.

Unstrapping her prosthetic leg, she let it fall to the floor, then straddled me, balancing herself with her strong hands.

"Say it's okay," she said.

She took me in her hand and moved me so that I could feel the soft hair, the warmth, the wetness waiting for me.

"Tell me you want me, want to be inside me."

"I ... I ..."

She began rubbing herself with the tip, moaning as she did.

"Say my name and I'll put you inside me."

I started to, but then hesitated.

"God, I've wanted you so long," she said. "So long. Say my name. Say aloud who you want to make love to."

"Ruth Ann?" I said. "It's you?"

"Yes."

"I can't."

"What? What'd you say?"

"I can't. I can't. I love Lauren. I can only be with her."

She moved her hand and slid down on me, arching her back, tossing her head back, letting out a breathless "Oh God" as she did.

"Stop," I said. "I only want Lauren."

"Lauren's dead. You can't have her. You can only have me now."

Meeting you has saved me. Being with you has caused me to wake up. I can only describe as divine. Please don't ever stop loving me that same way. You and I were always out of time, weren't we? We'll have eternity. All my love, all of me, Your Lauren

"No. Stop."

I realized then how much my abdomen was hurting, the pain searing, as if I were being stabbed over and over.

"Ruth Ann," I said. "It's no good. Get off me now."

"No. I know this is right. Just give in to it, soldier. I won't stop. I won't."

With far more force than I should have, I reached up with my arm and swept her away, slinging her flying across the coffee table and sprawling onto the floor, objects thudding, glass breaking, her crying.

38

"Good morning."

I awoke on the couch with Ruth Ann smiling down on me.

"Morning," I said.

I tried to sit up. It took some effort.

"I've gotta go check in with Clip," I said.

"We gonna talk about last night?" she said.

"Sure," I said. "I'm sorry. I've stayed far longer than I should have. I'm sorry I—"

"Don't be," she said. "It was my fault, fella. Not yours."

"I'll move out today," I said. "I don't have to hide out anymore."

"I want to pretend it never happened. Okay? I want you to accept my apology and then let's wipe the whole thing from our minds."

"Okay," I said, nodding.

"I really am sorry, pal," she said, and though she still looked like Lauren, she was back to sounding like her old self. "Oh, but one thing before we forget about the whole thing."

"Yeah?"

"I told you, didn't I? I knew you could get an ah ... Huh? How about that?"

I was so torn up about what happened, it hadn't even really registered that I could have done it, that I wasn't as wounded as I thought. I worked in a way I never thought I would again. It was incredible, and I'd be thrilled about it if the only woman I'll ever want weren't dead.

"Okay. So, again, I'm sorry. Now let's forget the whole thing."

"Forgotten," I said.

"And you don't have to rush to move out. Doesn't have to be today."

"Yes it does. I should've already. I'm sorry about that."

"Don't be. And don't be in such a rush to get out of here that you don't let me finish my one job and help you catch the killer. 'Cause I'm almost done."

"With?"

She nodded toward a folder on the kitchen table. "Gathering all the info and pictures on the girls that were killed. Will finish today. They could all be sisters."

"Oh yeah?"

"Yeah," she said. "And they're just your type."

When Ruth Ann dropped me off in front of the police station to get the car Harry left for me, I discovered it wasn't there.

I had been determined not to use it, but now that I was leaving Ruth Ann's and didn't want to borrow her car any longer, I had decided to take him up on the loan of it for a day or two.

But maybe it was too late. Had I waited too long?

I inquired inside and learned that it had been towed. I then took a cab to the impound lot, where they refused to release it to me.

"This car's registered to Panama City State Bank," a fat man with a nub of cigar sticking out of the corner of his mouth said.

"Your name's nowhere on it, pal."

"Tell you what—" I began.

"Look, fella, I sympathize. I do. But I know what you're doing. You think you're the first?"

He was sweaty and in need of a haircut, the stubble on his face and chin drawing attention to all the fat on his neck.

"What am I doing?"

"Trying to get your car back."

"Exactly."

"They repossessed it and now you're trying to steal it back from 'em."

"It's not like that. I'm working for the president of the bank. He provided the car. Call the bank. Ask the mayor."

"If you think I'm gonna spend my day callin'—"

"Or call Captain Folsom. He can tell you. Or let me borrow your phone and I'll do it."

"Knock yourself out."

I did, and in fifteen minutes I was pulling out of the lot in the black Ford registered to Panama City State Bank—which is where I drove it.

"Did you hear they found another one of those poor girls last night?" Harry asked.

We were in his office at the bank, which is where he asked me to come when I called for him to authorize me picking up the car.

I nodded.

The office was spacious and plush and filled with heavy masculine mahogany furniture. The chairs were upright and uncomfortable.

"I've just become mayor and something like this is happening. It won't do, Jimmy. It won't do. And I don't just mean how it looks politically. I mean it's my job to take care of this town."

I had nothing for that so I didn't respond.

Harry was puffing on a pipe, and the smoke filling his office had the sweet aroma of toasted marshmallows and warm vanilla.

"Police chief tells me the only real lead they got you gave them."

I shrugged.

"I know you're busy, but I'd like to hire you to help find the killer. And to help me with some security. I'm getting death threats. I don't mind telling you I'm frightened. I truly am. Now, I wouldn't want you to stop searching for Lauren's killers. Could you do both?"

"You mean all three?"

"Well, yes. All three."

"With some help."

"I'll pay you whatever you want. Name your price."

I thought about putting more crisp hundreds in Clip's pocket and a few in my own and it made me smile.

"Well?"

I named my price, which I thought was a little on the high side, but obviously that, like everything else, is relative, because he paid me out of his pocket.

39

When I finally got to De Grasse's place, Clip was gone.
It didn't take me long to figure out why.

Butch was in his squad car, windows down, smoking, and generally looking bored.

The sun was directly overhead, the late November day bright and clear. The temperature was hovering in the low fifties, but the wind off the water made it seem colder.

I was just going to turn around, but he waved me over. I pulled into the spot next to him, my car facing the opposite of his, and rolled down the window.

"Jimmy."

"Butch."

"What're you doing?"

"Looking for someone."

"Misplace your nigger again?"

Ignoring him, I asked, "Any sign of De Grasse?"

He shook his head. "He ain't comin' back here. This is a complete waste."

"Well, they picked the right man for that."

"Fuck you, Riley. Acting all high and mighty now. Don't think you're untouchable. Way I see it, your neck is still in the noose."

"I have no doubt that's the way you see it," I said. "Long as you're wearing a badge I'm sure it's true."

"Yeah, well, don't forget it."

A few boats bobbed in the bay, a few gulls swooped around, but there was no sign of other people as far as I could see in any direction.

"You thought any more about what might've happened to Pete?" I asked.

"Think about it all the time. He was my partner for God's sake. Nothing new has come to mind. Why?"

"Everywhere I look's a dead end," I said. "I really thought Howell and Walt must have done something to him when he got there, but now I'm not so sure."

"Oh yeah? Why's that?"

"Just think they were probably gone by the time he got there. What if he never even made it? You looked into any of his old cases? Any threats? Anybody get out that he put away?"

Butch frowned. "Just thought it was you. Or maybe that fat fuck Howell. Haven't looked any further."

"I really think that'd be a good use of your time," I said. "I know how you hate wasting it."

"Somebody squawked," Pat Newton, the chief of police, was saying, "and tomorrow it'll be splashed all over the front page of the paper."

He was a smallish man with a halo of white hair around a shiny dome head sitting in a huge chair behind an enormous desk.

I was standing outside his office, but could hear everything being said. Lewis was inside with him and Henry Folsom. I was providing security for the mayor and was grateful for the thin walls and door and the raised voices.

It was later that afternoon, and I was tagging along with

Harry in case anyone tried to make good on the threats they'd made. I had still not heard from Clip and he wasn't at his house when I stopped by before meeting Harry at the bank.

"Just make our job that much harder," Folsom said.

Newton's secretary, a plain woman pretending not to be listening, had switched from typing to something less noisy not long after the meeting began. Her name was Penny and her pale skin bore no makeup and her dishwater blond hair was pulled back into a long ponytail.

"We gotta get out in front of it," Harry said. "Issue a statement or hold a press conference. We can't look like we're caught off guard, can't seem like we've been lying to the public."

"We haven't," Folsom said.

"Well, maybe not, but you've certainly been withholding a hell of a lot. And I'm talking about how it looks. That's what matters, how the public will perceive it."

"What matters is catching the sick sex killer," Folsom said. "Not much else."

"That's something we won't get to do if we lose our jobs," Lewis said, then looking at Newton continued, "You know you'll be the first to get sacked. It's years until I'm up for reelection. I can weather this, but not you. I'm trying to help 'cause I want this maniac caught and I think you, your department, has the best chance of doing that. To bring in someone new now to take over would be ... disastrous."

"I agree," Newton said. "How can we ensure that doesn't happen?"

"We've got to catch him," Folsom said. "And soon. And not just to save our jobs, but because of what he's doing to our young ladies."

"Of course. Nobody's arguing we shouldn't do all we can to catch him. And I trust you are. But it hasn't resulted in his arrest yet. Hell, if it weren't for Jimmy we wouldn't have any leads at all. All I'm saying is that while you're trying to catch him, we've got to get out in front of this where the public is concerned. Let's attack it head on. Release a statement, hold a press conference, hell, I'll even pay for a full-page ad in the paper to tell our side of the story."

"Who you think their source is?" Folsom asked.

"Riley?" Newton asked.

Penny shot me a surreptitious glance. I held a finger up to my lips. She quickly looked away, acting as if she hadn't seen me.

"No," Folsom said. "No way."

"Of course it's not Jimmy," Harry said. "Probably that little puff who runs the gallery."

"Yeah. You're right."

"I think you should use Jimmy," Harry said. "He's the only one to come up with anything so far."

"Isn't he too busy guarding your body, Mr. Mayor?"

"I'm serious."

"I can't have a civilian working one of our cases."

"Then give him his old job back."

"Harry, he's missing an arm—and he's still a suspect in a murder investigation."

Penny was far less surreptitious this time. I made a gun with my thumb and forefinger and pointed it at her. Her pale skin flushed a deep pink and she grabbed at the charm on her necklace as if it were a talisman.

"Don't get me wrong," Newton continued. "I appreciate what he did. But now all we need to do is locate this De Grasse fella."

Delton Rogers saw me as he passed by in the hall and came into Penny's office.

"Hiya, Jimmy," he said, looking confused. "Whatta you doing?"

"Trailing the mayor. You?"

"Ran that tag for you."

"Yeah? Thanks."

"Car is registered to Panama City State Bank. What's that mean?"

"Probably stolen. Maybe a repo. Could still have had it from back when he worked for Mr. Lewis. I'll ask him. Any news on De Grasse?"

He shook his head. "But it's just a matter of time."

I smiled. "Hope you're right."

"Usually am," he said. "Well, see you around, pal."

"Thanks again for the info."

40

"I need to talk to you about something sensitive," I said.

"Okay," Harry said.

We were in the backseat of his car, the partition between us and his driver closed, Harry looking old and tired, his face flushed, his breath smelling of alcohol.

"But before I do ... remember how I told you I had seen Walt?"

"Yeah?"

"The car he was driving was registered to your bank."

"Really? Are you certain?"

"I am."

"I'll check when we get back to see if one's missing. Of course he may still have the one he drove back when he pretended to work for me. I guess that's possible too. I don't really keep up with those sorts of things very well. I'll find out and let you know. Hate to think he has anything of mine."

"Okay. Thanks."

"So, on to the sensitive topic," he said.

"I know a while back you hired Ray to follow Lauren."

"That was a long time ago," he said, sounding both defensive and dismissive. "What about it?"

"You suspected her of ... having a relationship with ... someone else."

"Not exactly, no," he said. "What's this about?"

The driver drove around downtown as we talked, moving slowly in the traffic—passing the Cove Hotel on Cherry, the Sherman on Fifth, the Cove Gardens on Watson Bayou, the National Guard Armory on Sixth, the post office at the corner of Fifth and Jenks.

"I'm trying to find all those responsible for her death," I said. "In the process I've uncovered a few things that made me realize I don't know as much as I thought I did."

"Like what?"

"Do you know who Lauren was seeing?"

"You mean besides you?"

I hesitated, and before I could say anything, he spoke again.

"Lauren was like a daughter to me. You know that. I knew she had lovers—or that she might. I know how much you meant to her, how much you meant to each other. I didn't hire Ray to find out if she was having a relationship so much as find out who it was with. I was planning to make my bid for mayor and I was trying to figure out what I'd be up against when I did."

"Do you remember any names?"

"Never heard any. Decided I was running either way so figured it was a waste of time and money. If something came up or out, we'd deal with it then."

"So you never got any—"

"Never got anything. And I'm glad I didn't."

"Forget what Ray found or didn't. Do you know of anyone? Did you suspect anyone?"

"Just you ... and ... the priest."

"Father Keller?"

He nodded.

"I know how much both of you meant to her, how much y'all did for her. I appreciate you both more than you'll ever know. You don't have any children, but if you ever do you'll know what I'm talking about. Anyone who is good and kind to your child becomes a treasure to you."

I thought about what he had said.

"It makes no difference to me," he said, "but based on her letter and what I've learned about my extraordinary girl, I don't think she was intimate with the priest. He also was like a father to her." He laughed as he realized what he had said. "In more ways than one."

I was pretty sure Lauren's relationship with Keller had not been sexual. So who had given her the disease that had killed her? Would I ever find out? And, if I was going to, how?

When we reached Panama City State Bank on Harrison, the driver pulled up so that Harry was next to the curb.

He started to slide forward on the seat, but stopped, hesitating there like that a moment.

"You okay?"

"I've wanted to be mayor of this town for as long as I can remember."

"Yeah?"

"But I'm just not sure I'm up to it."

"You're tired and—"

"There's just so much to it," he said. "I had no idea. And everybody's unhappy about something. I've just gotten in office and ... It doesn't matter. You're right. I'm just tired. I need a drink. Let's just get to my office."

"Okay. You ready?"

He nodded.

I got out, walked around the back of the car and opened the door for him.

The sidewalk was as crowded with pedestrians as Harrison

was with vehicles, and we paused for a moment to let a young mother pushing a large baby carriage pass by.

As we began walking, I glanced around, trying to keep my vision wide and unfocused, taking in as much as I could of the activity.

When we were about halfway between the car and the entrance to the bank, an unkempt man in gray trousers and a plain white T-shirt rushed around the end of a large gray bus idling in traffic, a handgun held up and out.

He had too long thick black hair and dark stubble on a pale face.

"We told you, Harry Lewis." he yelled in a thick Middle Eastern accent. "You will not escape our wrath."

Then he began firing.

The first round pierced the glass of the right side of the double doors and hit something solid inside.

Screams.

Panic.

Running.

Tripping.

Scattering.

Pandemonium.

The second round hit the brick on the right side of the bank front just a few inches from the head of the young mother.

The man was still twenty-five feet away and running. The chances of him hitting anything he meant to were slim.

Grabbing Harry across the chest, I brought my right leg around and swept his feet out from beneath him. Pushing him with my arm, I dropped him to the ground.

I then turned and placed myself between the young mother and the shooter as I reached in my coat for my gun.

The next round hit a fat business man exiting the bank in the back of the neck. He went down as blood began spurting from the wound.

That ratcheted up the panic and pandemonium a few more notches.

The shooter was on the sidewalk now less than twenty feet away, and as he saw me attempting to withdraw my weapon, he pointed his gun directly at me.

Awkwardly I fumbled to retrieve the revolver, but I had not yet cleared leather when the shooter's head exploded.

I turned toward the direction of the shot and saw Harry's driver, his door open, holding a gun of his own, using the roof of the car to steady his shot.

The shooter crumpled to the sidewalk, dropping his weapon, his right leg bent back beneath his body, which was now splayed across the cement, a halo of blood and brain matter around what was left of his head.

Panicking people continued to yell and scream and run, but the episode was over, and I helped Harry to his feet, realizing how much better the wound in my abdomen had been doing now that it was beginning to twinge again.

"You okay?" I asked.

A young serviceman in uniform knelt down beside the fat businessman and applied pressure to the wound in his neck while yelling for someone to call an ambulance.

"Yeah, just a little shaken up, but I'm fine."

I looked over at the driver and nodded.

He nodded back as he holstered his weapon.

There was nothing remarkable or distinguishing about him. He was just an average man, his black uniform making him even more nondescript.

"Thank you, Timothy," Harry said.

"I'm not sure you need me," I said. "Timothy has both arms and knows how to use them."

41

F ollowing the press conference and getting Harry in for the night, I arrived back at Ruth Ann's to find the house empty.

I had come to gather up the last of my things and get the information on the victims she had for me.

Unlike the other times I had returned to find her gone, there was no note letting me know where she was and how long she'd be.

Of course, not only was she not expecting me, but I was sure, despite what she said, she was still sore about what happened last night.

Before packing up everything, I decided to clean up and change, letting my mind soak in the details of the investigation the way my body was the water.

Later, as I pulled together my things, I came across Lauren's letter and sat down and began reading it again.

My Dearest Jimmy,

I have so much to say to you and such a short time to say it. If you're reading this, then chances are I died. Those chances are looking more and more likely these days, and I don't want that to happen without me getting to tell you just how much I love you.

I know you don't understand right now, but I do love you more deeply, more profoundly than you can imagine. I've never loved anyone like this, never been loved by anyone the way you have loved me. Even now, I know you love me. I hear it in every cruel, sarcastic remark, see it in your anger and frustration, have felt it in all the ways you've tried to help me lately without even knowing what's been going on.

Meeting you has saved me. Being with you has caused me to wake up. Our love, mine for you and yours for me, has forever changed me. And though it is us, from us, a part of us, it also is beyond us. Through you I've experienced a love that I can only describe as divine.

This experience has been overwhelming for me, and I know I have not handled it well. I'm so very sorry for that. I know you've not understood and that you've felt betrayed, rejected, abandoned. I can see why you would feel that way, but in my heart, in my actions, I have never done anything but love and care for you. I just wish now that I had done those things better.

Please forgive me. Please know how very deeply I love you. Please don't ever stop loving me that same way.

And do yourself a favor and look to the source of your love for me, my love for you. There is a reality beyond what we can see.

Forgive me. Forgive Harry. Forgive yourself.

Quit trying to save the world. Stop putting so much pressure on yourself. Do your best, which is plenty, then step back, let go, move on.

There's so much more I want to say, but I'm out of time. You and I were always out of time, weren't we?

But you know the big beyond I was talking about, the source of all love, it's a timeless place, and we'll be there together soon. Open yourself up to it. I'll be waiting for you there. Join me, Jimmy. When your time here is done—and don't rush it! There's no rush. We'll have eternity.

I just thought of something. This is all you need to do. You know the way you love me? Open yourself up to the source of that love and love yourself and others that same way. See you soon, my dear strong soldier.

All my love, all of me,

Your Lauren

When I finished, I wiped at the tears streaming from my eyes and just sat there—sat with her, with her words, with our love.

Eventually, I folded it back up, returned it to its envelope, and placed it back inside the priest's Bible.

As I put the Bible back in the box in the corner, Ruth Ann's file folder of information about the victims caught my eye, and I sat down at the table, opened it, and began flipping through it.

As she had indicated, the file was incomplete, but there was still plenty in it.

The first thing that struck me was how alike all the girls looked. It was true they had looked similar in death, but that was no comparison to the way they resembled one another in life.

Of the five victims so far, there were only three pictures, but the three that were there looked nearly identical, as if sisters— triplets even.

The wound in my abdomen began aching as my heart sank into it when I realized how much each victim looked like Lauren. Of course, none of them were quite as pretty, not quite as perfect, but their brown eyes and dark hair and sexy mouths and narrow arching eyebrows resembled Lauren's.

And then I saw the list of names and knew why.

I recognized two of them.

Lauren's words echoed in my mind.

"Of the infidelity cases you investigate, how many of the people turn out to be cheating? How many? I want to know."

It was her first visit to my office. Like so many others before her, she had come to hire me to see if her husband was cheating on her.

"So, of the cases you've worked, how many were guilty of cheating?" she asked.

"All of them," I said.

"I love my husband, Mr. Riley. Like a father. I'm not in love with him—not like a wife. I care about him a great deal. I owe him ... well, everything. But if I knew he had someone ... It would be a great comfort to me."

He had had someone—a few of them—the discovery of which helped us justify what we were doing.

I had followed Harry Lewis for his wife what seemed like a lifetime ago. I didn't remember everything about the case, but I distinctly recall the joy at uncovering his unfaithfulness and at least two of the names of the girls he was seeing—names that were on the list of victims.

42

I drove to Harry's in the car he had provided me beneath the light of a big moon, the bright night clear and cold.

I sped down Fifteenth, turned on Jenks, and took Sixth over to Beach, my mind racing far faster than I could make the car go.

What was Harry's connection to the victims? Had they all been his mistresses? Was he the killer? It was hard to imagine him doing what was done to those girls—his age and physical condition alone would seem to make it nearly impossible.

Was it a coincidence that two of the names on the list had a connection to him? It could be just the two, could be that the way they lived made them more vulnerable to coming in contact with men like Harry and the killer.

Harry could be involved and not be the killer, could be connected to him in some way.

Was this what Walt meant about me not having a clue about what was really going on?

And then it hit me. What if the car Walt was driving wasn't stolen? What if he was still working for Harry? What if he had been all along? Was that why he didn't leave town? Why he killed the others? But if that were true, he wouldn't have been helping Howell. And maybe he wasn't. Maybe he was just pretending to. Maybe it wasn't a double but a triple cross. Maybe there was even more to it than that and that's what he meant. Maybe I was stumbling around blindly in the dark even more than usual.

When I reached Harry's house on Beach Drive I found it empty and his car gone.

Breaking in, I decided to have a look around. There was nothing suspicious—except it looked as if no one really lived here.

Snatching up the phone, I dialed Delt.

He sounded like I woke him up.

"Jimmy? What is it?"

"I think Harry Lewis may be involved in the killings."

"What? The mayor? The man who freed you and you're now working for?"

"Yeah."

"You're an entertaining and unpredictable fella. I'll give you that. What makes you suspect Lewis?"

"At least two of the victims were his mistresses."

"That's it?"

"So far."

"That's pretty thin. Not saying it's nothing, but you're takin' a helluva risk accusing the mayor of something like that based on a distant connection to two of the girls."

"I know. I'm still looking into it."

"Where are you?"

"Harry's. He's not here. I'm poking around a bit 'til he gets back."

"You take chances, don't you, soldier? Damn man. Be careful. What do you want me to do?"

"Just wanted you to know. Maybe look into it a little on your own when you can."

"Will do. Now finish up and get out of there before he gets back."

I looked around some more, spending most of my time lingering with Lauren's things, which appeared to have been untouched, unmolested, exactly as they would have been when she left.

God, I ached for her, longed to be lingering with her instead of her things, just to be with her the way we once were, lost in each other, hidden from every other soul in the world on our island of intimacy.

In the back of the house, I stumbled upon the live-in housekeeper asleep in a chair in front of a small radio.

"God almighty, boy," she said. "You scared the life outta me."

"Sorry."

She was an older black woman, so thin she appeared emaciated.

"I'm—"

"I know who you are."

"I'm working for Har—Mr. Lewis. Helping with security. Do you know where he is?"

"No, sir. He gone most nights. Know he got another place somewhere, but don't know where it is. Stop stayin' here after Miss Lauren left."

"No idea where it is?"

"Not the first clue. He usually back first thing in the morning. Make it look like he was here all night. Eats his breakfast and gets ready for work."

"Thank you," I said. "Sorry again for scaring you."

As I turned to leave, the phone rang. I waited as she walked into the hall to answer it.

"If it's Har—Mr. Lewis, let me talk to him."

She didn't respond.

"Lewis residence." She paused for a moment, looked back at me, and said, "Yes, sir. He still here."

She then handed me the phone.

"Riley."

"Jimmy, it's Delt. We got another body. I think you might know her ... Ruth Ann Johnson."

43

As I raced down Eleventh toward Adrian's place, tremors ran the length of my body and I felt feverish.

This was my fault.

I should've never involved her, never asked for her help, never let her keep up the charade of my surrogate Lauren. I had unknowingly sent her out into the world to gather information about the victims while looking like one.

Thoughts of my guilt were interrupted by questions about the murderer. Where had they crossed paths? Was it Harry or De Grasse or someone else? Why display her in Adrian's show again? He took a hell of a risk coming back to it. Why? Why return to a place so recently crawling with cops?

"You sure you're up for this?" Delt asked.

He was waiting for me by his car at the curb in front of the dimly lit Victorian.

"You don't have to—"

"Yes I do. She on the third floor like the other?"

He nodded.

"Where is everybody?"

There were only two cars parked on the curb, and there didn't seem to be much activity taking place inside the house.

"I had them give us a minute. The rest of them will be here soon. If you want time alone with her ..."

The third-story room was still a wreck from being a crime scene the first time, the displays disturbed, disjointed, displaced.

There was very little left out in the middle of the floor, most things having been shoved toward the walls, but now in the center of the room a white silk sheet was draped over a body.

"You don't have to do this," Delt said.

"This the way you found her?"

He nodded. "I lifted the sheet, looked at her face, returned the sheet, called you."

"Where is Adrian?"

"Having a drink in the back room downstairs. He's shaken up but good."

I approached the body beneath the sheet.

"You sure?" he asked again.

"Yes. Quit asking me."

Kneeling down beside the body, I carefully took a corner of the sheet in my hand and pulled it back.

The first thing I saw was a shock of blond hair.

But even before I could register what was wrong with that, the blonde Nazi bitch who had tortured and threatened to eat me sprung up and jabbed a syringe into my neck, depressing the plunger immediately as she did, and just as immediately the paralysis set in and I crumpled to the floor.

"You didn't give him too much, did you?" Delt was saying.

"Ze drug is experimental. Zis is not exact scientific."

I was folded into the backseat of Delt's car. He was driving, and Christa, the tall, thin blonde woman with fine, short hair and jagged bangs who still haunted my dreams, was in the passenger seat.

She turned and looked down at me, her ice-blue soulless eyes beneath her razor-sharp eyebrows ghoulishly gleeful.

"Vell, you are avake. Zis is good. Sometime Nazi doctor drugs too strong for veak, vounded half-man like yourself."

"I took all you could give me last time, sister."

She laughed. "I had not even begun before you escaped. Besides, zis time you vill experience ze emotional torture as vell as ze physical. You vill die in more pain zan you zought possible and zen, as I promised, I vill eat you."

I felt thickheaded and slow, my mouth and throat parched. I couldn't move anything from the neck down, as if my entire body was asleep.

"What's your part in all this, Delt? You twisted motherfucker."

"Language, Mr. Riley," Christa said. "Language."

"I know you're not artistic, so what? You the cutter?"

"I do all ze surgery, zank you," Christa said.

"De Grasse is the artist," Delt said. "Or was."

"I operate," Christa said. "Flaxon displays."

"Was?" I asked.

"He's no longer with us."

"He began to get ... a bit demanding. Ve sent him a message," Christa said. "Razer zan straighten up, he takes ze money and runs."

"What was the message?"

"You saw it," Delt said.

"I did?"

"We shoved it right up his ass," he said.

"Ve put his real art inside his faux art installation—brought ze cops right to his doorstep."

"Adrian is De Grasse?" I asked.

Delt nodded.

"The place on the water ..."

"A decoy. Buy him some time if anyone got too close."

"Zen he tried to take out ze boss."

"You were there for that too," Delt said, and I could hear the smile in his voice.

"The attack on Harry," I said.

Delt said, "For a moment there it looked like the boss was gonna miss his chance to make you pay for what you done."

"Which is what?" I asked. "What have I done?"

"You took another man's wife, pal. It's what led to all this. Every bit of this is your fault."

"So all that stuff about loving her like a daughter was bullshit?"

"Whatta you think? She shouldn't've married him if she didn't want him to fuck her. She could spend his money but couldn't suck his dick? Come on, fella, you know that ain't jake."

"So you're doing this to help a man avenge his wife's infidelity?" I asked.

"Anybody ever put his hands on my wife would lose his hands and a lot more, mister. You can bet the one hand you got left on that."

"At least be honest," I said. "You've been bought. You were for sale and you got bought."

"Ungrateful, unfaithful whore," he said, as if he hadn't heard me.

"Just out of curiosity, what was your price?"

He didn't say anything.

"Ve have all become very, very rich," Christa said.

"For killing innocent young women?"

"Innocent?" Delt said, expelling a sharp burst of humorless laughter. "It was just a few filthy whores."

And then I saw it. That was it. Harry had to be the one to infect Lauren. He had found young women who looked like her and at least one of them gave it to him—or maybe he already had it and gave it to them. Either way, they had to be silenced. Couldn't take a chance on them coming out to expose the newly elected mayor.

"Did he rape her?" I asked.

"You can't rape your wife, pal. What you did, that was rape. Not what a husband does."

Goddamn but I had been wrong about Harry. Lauren had too —and it had cost her her life.

"He looks so sad," Christa said. "Ve are feeling pathetic, no?"

"Just realizes he's not as smart as he thinks he is and he knows this is it," he said. Then looking in the rearview mirror, said, "And your nigger can't save you this time."

I didn't respond, just wondered again where Clip was.

"You're always a step behind, Jimmy," he said. "Wanna hear something funny? When you were talking to Butch, your nigger was in the trunk of his car."

"Butch in on this too?"

He shook his head. "Didn't even know. Dumb son of a bitch. I put him in there. It was my car. He's in there now."

"Butch?"

"What? No. The nigger. Who the hell knows where Butch is? Who the hell cares?"

"Maybe if you yell loud enough he'll hear you—if he's still breathin'. He's been in there a while though. I would tell you to tap out a message to him if you could move anything but your mouth."

I could feel a faint sensation in my arm and hand and in my feet, as if they were beginning to wake up, though there were no prickly pins and needles.

"What about Pete?" I said.

"Pete? What about him?"

"What'd you do to him?"

"Don't know anything about Pete. Sure as shit didn't do anything to him."

"Okay, ve are close now," Christa said, reaching back and covering my face with a chemical-soaked cloth. "Time for you to go night-night, Mr. Riley. I bid you bad nightmares. See you when you vake up in hell."

44

When I regained consciousness, I was strapped to a front-row seat in a small but plush theater. The rich lavender curtain was closed so I couldn't see what was on the stage, but as I craned my neck around, I could see that the walls of the room were decorated with surrealist art and quotes and the back had an installation not unlike the one on the third floor of Adrian Fromerson's or Flaxon De Grasse's house.

Compared to the art there, the work hanging here was far more surreal, far more sexual, far more violent.

"Ready for the show?" Harry asked, stepping out of a door at the right side of the stage. "I can't tell you how long I've waited for this."

"For what?"

"The singular pleasure of watching you suffer and die," he said as he walked over and stood before me.

"Oh that."

"That's perfect," he said. "Attempt to be cavalier. That will make watching you break even better. You are about to experience more emotional, psychological, and physical pain than you ever thought possible, and long before you die you will break and beg like a baby for its mother."

"This doesn't strike you as a little extreme?" I said. "All this because your wife who was young enough to be your grand-daughter had an affair."

"Had an affair? Had an affair? It was far more than a goddamn affair. She loved you so fuckin' much she found God. Just an affair. She loved you like she had never loved anyone. Ever. Think about all I had done for her, all I had given her—everything. Everything. All I asked of her was love and respect and affection. And what did I get? I got treated like a leper while you—you got everything. I gave everything. You were given everything."

"She didn't begin a relationship with me until she knew you were involved with other women."

"Involved? Involved? I wasn't involved with other women. I was fucking whores who looked like her. Why? Because the whore I had saved and raised and educated and made my wife wouldn't give me anything in return. I repulsed her. I could see it in her eyes. Me. After all I had done. I contracted syphilis. All because of her. Do you understand? She made me get the damn disease of a fuckin' whore. Me. The president of Panama City State Bank. The mayor of Panama City. Well, I made good and goddamn well she got it too."

"And used Walt and the others to make sure she didn't get treatment."

"I wasn't trying to keep her from treatment. I was trying to get her to turn to me. But she never did."

I didn't say anything, just thought about how this sick old man had taken everything from me. Everything.

"Enough of that," he said. "It's time for the show. Okay, let's see. The only thing you need to know is that everything you're about to witness is going to happen to you—as soon as you get feeling back in your body. Can't have it not hurt, now can we?"

He sat down beside me as the house lights dimmed and the stage lights and curtain came up.

The stage was completely white. Blindingly bright beneath the theater lights.

Ruth Ann's nude body was mounted upright, spread-eagle to a giant white X with white cables that bit into her flesh. Beside her, in white operating scrubs, gown, gloves, and a cap with a red swastika on it, Christa held a large power saw.

"Let me hear you be cavalier now, tough guy," Harry said.

"Please," I said. "I'll do anything you want. Torture me for years. I won't even resist. Just let her go. She has nothing to do with this. Please. I'm begging you. What can I do?"

"Nothing. You are powerless. You have nothing to offer. What you are offering—being tortured and killed—is what is going to happen to you. All you can do is watch this happen and then have it happen to yourself. How does that feel? Think about how I felt when no matter what I did, I was powerless to win Lauren's love. There was nothing I could do to save her from a two-bit dick like you. Powerless."

On stage, Christa was looking at what was left of Ruth Ann's missing leg. "Someone beat me to zis one."

"Jimmy," Ruth Ann said. "Please. Help me. Jimmy."

"I'm so sorry," I said. "They've paralyzed me. I can't move."

"Plus he is strapped down," Harry said. "I assure you, he cannot save you. No one can."

"Why are you doing this?" she said. "WHY? Please don't. I'll do anything. I'll ... please, anything you want. Just don't do this. Please."

"I'm sorry, my dear, but your fate is sealed. You can thank Jimmy for that."

"Oh God. Jimmy. Please. I'm so scared."

"As she should be," he said to me. "We've given her nothing. She will feel every slice of flesh and muscle, every rip and tear, every nick and break and cut of bone."

Christa turned on the saw as Ruth Ann began to squirm and scream and I continued to plead with Harry.

The power tool was unbelievably loud in the small theater, sounding as horrific as anything I had ever heard except for Ruth Ann's screams.

Christa began with the left arm.

Ruth Ann tried to wiggle it away, but it was strapped down too tight.

Lining up the blade at just below the shoulder, Christa prepared to make her first cut.

"PLEASE," Ruth Ann screamed. "OH GOD. NO. PLEASE. NO. I'LL DO—"

Lowering the saw on the spot she had picked out, Christa's white outfit was instantly splattered with blood. The blade quickly and easily ripped through the skin, muscles, and tendons, and only took a little longer to grind through the bone.

I have never heard screams like the ones coming out of Ruth Ann's torture-contorted face—not ever—and when the saw stopped, they only grew worse.

I knew she was in shock, and I knew soon she would stop screaming, but for the moment it was bad. It was as bad as anything could ever be.

"Are you crying?" Harry said.

I hadn't realized I was.

Even before the horror began I had begun putting distance between myself and what was about to happen, and if I hadn't, the shock that soon came would have done it for me, but I guess neither were strong enough to stop the involuntary tears at what I was witnessing.

"That's so sweet."

With her arm strapped to the upper crossbar of the X, Ruth Ann resembled the other victims, their limbs severed, but only a little space between them.

Images of the friendship we had shared came unbidden.

Knocking back bottles of Schlitz at Nick's. The way she had always worried about me. I thought about every kindness, the way she had cared for me, nursed me back to health, her gentleness and strength and bravery. How many boys were alive today because of her work in the war?

"Never thought you'd feel this way, did you?" Harry asked. "Never thought anything like this was possible."

"Nothing can compare to losing Lauren," I said. "Nothing. You should remember that while you're doing all this. There's nothing you can do to me that can come close to the pain of losing the great love of my life—the woman who loved me like no other."

"Oh, we'll see about that. We're just getting started. And I've had a lot of time to plan this. You'll see."

"I love you, Jimmy," Ruth Ann said in a small, sad, childlike voice. They were the last words she ever spoke.

Soon Christa went back to work, continuing until she and the saw and the stage were covered with Ruth Ann's blood, until Ruth Ann was too weak to do anything but whimper. She removed her good leg first, then her other arm, then the stump of her missing leg. Ruth Ann was so pathetic, so sad and spent, and the only good thing, the only grace, was that she was in such shock that she was past the point of feeling much of anything and very soon she would be dead.

The brilliant white of the stage beneath the flood of bright light caused the dark red of Ruth Ann's blood to be all the more astounding, the gruesome scene too much to process, too revolting to be real. And yet it was. It was all too real.

45

Ruth Ann was dead now. Now, Christa would turn her attention to me.

"He should be regaining some feeling by now," she said from the stage. "See if he is."

"How?" Harry asked.

"Stab him in ze leg. Just not too deep. Don't want him bleeding out before I get to work on him."

She withdrew a knife from a tray near her and tossed it to Harry. It clattered on the floor and slid over not far from his feet.

I was beginning to get some feeling back, my limbs waking, but I had to convince him I wasn't. I even felt as though I might be able to move soon, but I couldn't let him know that. Could I act like I couldn't feel the stab? Was that possible? I prepared myself.

He picked up the knife, which had traces of Ruth Ann's blood on it, and poked at my leg.

It hurt, but I didn't respond.

"You feel that?" he asked.

"Yeah, it's killin' me. Please stop. You're hurting me so bad."

"Well?" Christa yelled from the stage.

"Nothing yet."

"Make sure he's not faking. Stab him good and hard. Just try not to go too deep."

He did as she said, driving the sharp knife at least two inches into the top of my leg.

Tears came to my eyes, but were masked by the ones already there.

"Still dead."

"Goddamn, I hope ze dose didn't do permanent damage. Hate for him not to feel zis. Go ahead and unstrap him. Ve can get him all set up vhile ve vait to see if he's gonna vake up to die. Call Rogers. Ve're gonna need his help."

"Where is Delt?" I asked.

"Doesn't have the stomach for this part. Need someone keeping an eye out for Flaxon anyway."

"What's Flaxon's deal?"

"Doesn't play well with others."

"What'd you expect from an anarchist?"

As Harry came around behind me and began loosening the straps that held me to the chair, I slumped as if I were unable to hold myself up.

"We don't need him anymore anyway," he said.

"Already killed all the girls you infected?"

"The only thing left is for him to be shot to death by the police when they try to apprehend him."

"The police or Delt?"

"I've got a few friends on the force."

"What are your plans for me?"

"I haven't told you? I'm slipping in my old age. We're gonna strip you naked and mount you facedown on top of your bloody slut just like you're fucking her, then Christa's gonna slice you apart too, and just before you die, I'm gonna whisper something in your ear that will be the pièce de résistance."

"What could you possibly tell me that I don't already know?" I said. "That you raped Lauren and gave her your disease? That you killed her? That you and your little Nazi bitch are the sickest fuckin' people on the planet?"

"You'll see."

When he loosened the last of the straps, I crumpled to the floor as if I were unable to do otherwise.

"Get Delt," Harry said. "Let's get him strung up and get on with it."

I craned my head up off the floor and looked around. Christa was disappearing off the back part of the stage, calling for Delt as she did. Then Harry's expensive shoes were beside me.

"She really did look like Lauren a bit, didn't she?" Harry said. "'Cept for the eyes. We'll keep those closed so you can still pretend it's Lauren you're fuckin' up there."

"He's not out zere," Christa said.

"What? Is his car gone?"

"It's still zere."

"Then he's around. Probably went to take a piss. Don't panic."

"I'm not pani—"

That was all she got out before her head exploded and her blood and brain matter shot out, joining Ruth Ann's on the stage.

I had no idea who had shot her or what was going on, but I knew now was my moment.

I swept my legs around and knocked Harry's out from underneath him. As soon as he hit the ground, I was on top of him, wrestling the knife out of his hand, cutting myself in the process.

As soon as I had it away from him, I slid the sharp blade across his fat neck, slicing open his jugular, his warm blood spurting out, spraying me, soaking his shirt.

He grabbed at the gape in the side of his neck, his wide eyes panicky and pained.

"You deserve a lot worse," I said.

I heard footsteps on the stage and looked up to see who it was.

"I should kill you for robbing me of the satisfaction of killing him," Flaxon De Grasse said. "Or I could let you live because you killed him—you know, the enemy of my enemy ... Look at the mess this bitch made."

He shook his head and walked off, disappearing, as Christa had before, at the rear of the stage.

Harry was calmer now. He was trying to say something.

"Last words," I said. "What do you have to say?" "... was going to tell you," he said, "... just ... before you ... died. Guess ... it will be before ... I do."

"Then you better hurry," I said.

"Come closer," he said.

I did.

"Lauren's alive," he said.

My mind reeled as I was rocked back by those two little words.

"What?"

"I had her declared ... DOA ... took her far ... far away ... got her ... best care possible ... nursed her back ... Wanted you ... both to know ... I knew ... wanted you to suffer ... to be tortured and ... die horrible deaths ... She will. No one knows who she is ... you will ... never find ... her. I mean ... never. You ... helped kill her ... again ... You just ... killed the only person ... on the planet ... who knows ... who and ... where ... she ..."

And with that, he died.

46

E arly the next morning with no sleep and no peace, I stood before Lauren's grave, Clip on one side, Henry Folsom on the other.

The headstone and earth removed, the coffin was now being raised.

What did I want more? Harry to have been lying or telling the truth? Was it possible she really was alive? Did I dare to hope? Was I wishing a horrible fate on her if I did?

Clip was in bad shape, having nearly died in Delt's trunk, but he had insisted on being here. I had never met a more loyal man.

Like Christa, Delt had been killed by Flaxon, who had disappeared. He was dangerous and on the loose. There was still no clue as to what happened to Pete either, but all I cared about was whether the mortal remains of my love were inside the box about to be opened or if she, like hope, remained here with me on this side of the big beyond.

And then with no fanfare or even a dramatic pause, the casket was opened.

Decay.

Decomposition.

Death.

The body inside was degraded and deteriorated, the rancid stench causing all of us to recoil.

I felt my stomach lurch, as the cemetery began to whirl around me.

"Look," Clip said, as the lid was removed the rest of the way.

I did.

And that's when I realized the reason for the advanced stage of decomposition. The body had not been embalmed and prepared for burial.

Because it wasn't Lauren. It was Pete.

I had never, not in all my life, been so happy to see a friend dead. I'd feel bad for him later and even worse for how I felt, but right now all I experienced was relief ... relief and the slightest glimmer of hope.

"It's not her," Clip said.

"It's Pete Mitchell," Folsom said. "Poor Pete."

She's alive. Lauren's alive.

"We'll find her," they said simultaneously, as if hearing my thoughts.

"Yes we will," I said. "Yes. We. Will."

START THE NEXT NOVEL NOW!

Turn the page to start the next Jimmy Riley Noir Novel — THE GIRL AT THE END OF THE LONG DARK NIGHT.

THE GIRL AT THE END OF THE LONG
DARK NIGHT - CHAPTER 1

Night was falling fast.

Clip and I were driving east toward Tallahassee, the final flare of fading sunburst burning out behind the pines lining the horizon behind us.

The descending darkness blanketing the earth seemed to be settling in, as if for a long black night––the kind where bad people operate with impunity, and in which bad things happen. Dark deeds that, like death, can't be undone.

Though one-armed and injured, I was driving––and not just because Clip couldn't see for shit at night with his one eye, but because he didn't want to be mistaken for my chauffeur.

We were searching for Lauren Lewis––something I had been doing my entire life.

Earlier in the day, weak, weary, and without sleep, we had stood alongside Henry Folsom, the best cop I knew and my old boss, over an open wound in the earth that was supposed to be Lauren's grave.

Headstone and hard dirt removed, coffin raised to reveal she wasn't inside.

Now, once again, I was in search of her, bumbling around in the dark trying to find her.

Her bent banker husband's final words still haunted me, echoing like the demented taunts of a madman in the claustrophobic chamber that was my mind.

Spoken the moment after I slit his throat, his life spilling out of him onto the floor, he had harshly whispered with the voice of death, " . . . was going to tell you just . . . before you . . . died. Guess . . . will be before . . . I do . . . Lauren's alive . . . I had her declared . . . DOA . . . took her far . . . far away . . . got her . . . best care possible . . . nursed her back . . . Wanted you . . . both to know . . . I knew . . . wanted you to suffer . . . to be tortured and . . . die horrible deaths . . . she will. No one knows who she is . . . you will . . . never find . . . her. I mean . . . never. You . . . helped kill her . . . again . . . you just . . . killed the only person . . . on the planet . . . who knows . . . who and . . . where . . . she—

As if knowing what I was thinking, Clip said, "Just 'cause Harry say she alive don't mean she is."

I didn't say anything.

He had his eye patch off and the mangled scar of socket was jarring.

"Just 'cause she not the one in that box don't mean she not in some box somewhere," he continued. "Know you ain't wantin' to hear it. Hell, I ain't wantin' to be sayin' it, but . . ."

He was right and I knew it.

I glanced over at him, at the narrow boniness inside the too loose suit.

"Then why you keep sayin' it?" I asked.

"'Cause you needs to hear it," he said.

I shook my head.

"You gots to prepare for—"

"Already lost her twice. That hasn't prepared me. There is no preparing. Nothing I can do. Nothing in this world could make it any less unbearable if I find out . . . if she's really . . . There's nothing else I can do."

"What if you never know for sure?" he said.

"Won't stop 'til I do."

We fell silent a moment—something I was grateful for.

The rural road was flat and straight and desolate, our solitary car the only vehicle, its half headlights made even fainter by the fog.

Thanks to Henry Folsom, we not only had a full tank of gas, but ration tickets to spare.

To conserve rubber for the war effort, I was supposed to be keeping it under thirty-five. I was doing nearly double that.

I thought of Lauren, of just how much I loved her, wanted her, needed her, of how I had to find her, of how I couldn't think of anything else.

Since the death of my dad when I was a kid, the only time I had felt safe, connected, and truly happy was when I had been with Lauren—and I had never, not in my entire life, felt as loved or in love, as possessing or possessed.

"Nothing matters but finding her," I said. "Nothing. What-ifs don't matter. Whether Harry was telling the truth doesn't matter. Nothing. Can't do anything to change whether I'm gonna find her dead or alive. All I can do is find her. Won't stop until I do and I'll do anything I have to."

"Anything, huh?"

"Those aren't just words," I said.

"I know you," he said. "I know they's shit you won't do."

"Not this time. Not when—"

"You'a beat up a bitch?"

I nodded.

He shook his head. "You wouldn't even slap hell outta one and you talkin' 'bout beatin' a bitch up."

"There's nothing I won't do."

"They's plenty you won't do," he said. "And that what worries me. What always worry me with you."

"Clip, I'm telling you--"

"You tellin' me what? That you'a cut a bitch? Sucker punch a stiff? Back-shoot a bastard? Kill a kid? Shee-it. They's plenty you won't do. Don't tell me they ain't."

I didn't respond.

Beyond the windows on both sides, silent trees streaked by like black lines on black paper, so impressionistic as to seem imaginative.

"Ain't sayin' it wrong. Hell, it part of why I even associate with your white ass. But don't say it ain't so. Knowing what you'a do and not do the difference between--"

"There a point to all this?"

"Not everybody cut out for every kind of work."

"You think I'm not up for this?"

"Think you needs to be clear on what you up for and what you ain't."

"I'm clear," I said.

"So shut the hell up, Clip," he said, smiling, his large bright white teeth seeming to light up the car. "Be seen and not heard like some docile house nigger."

"Something like that, yeah," I said with a small smile of my own.

"I can do that," he said.

"The hell you can."

He smiled again. Even bigger this time.

When Clip smiled with genuine amusement he looked like a mischievous young boy. Charming. Irrepressible. Full of himself.

We were both in bad shape, having run afoul of a Nazi nurse named Christa, a serial sex killer named Flaxon De Grasse, and various members of their twisted little surrealism society, and the moment of levity, the chance to smile, and the slight release of tension, was welcome and briefly buoying.

Maybe Clip was right. Maybe my moral code was a liability in looking for Lauren. Maybe I wasn't up for what would inevitably have to be done. I certainly wasn't physically.

I was useless enough without my right arm, but to also be injured, to be so completely depleted and thoroughly spent, to be banged up and bruised, to have an abdominal wound from getting gut shot actually seeping through the bandages at the moment, meant I couldn't look out for myself let alone save Lauren, but it didn't matter. I couldn't stop, could do nothing but what I was doing. No matter how many moral, emotional, and physical limitations I had to do it with.

"I've got to do this," I said.

"I know," he said, "and not just 'cause you done tol' me a few hundred times."

"Wasn't finished."

"Beg pardon. Please proceed."

"I've got to, but you don't. I know you think you owe me, but you don't. Never did."

"You think I tryin' to square the Dixon thing?"

A year or so back, when I was still part of PCPD, a couple of cops got the goods on Clip––something they'd been trying to do for a while. Wasn't much to it––some stolen merchandise Clip had little or nothing to do with––but that didn't matter. The two cops, Whitfield and Dixon, were just looking for a way in and they found it. Stolen merchandise was just their invite. Word was Clip had been sleeping with Dixon's wife. And I could tell by the way they were working the case they had no intention of taking it to trial. What they did intend was to tuck Clip in all nice and cozy to sleep the big sleep––probably making it look like he was killed trying to escape.

I had intervened and stopped them, and Clip had acted like he owed me ever since.

"The thought had occurred to me, yeah," I said.

"Well, I ain't. Least not the way you think."

"Oh yeah?"

"Yeah," he said, shaking his head. "I always be thinkin' you smarter than what you really is."

I laughed. "You're not the first to make that mistake."

We fell silent a moment.

In the dim spill of our half headlights, deer could be seen grazing the cold, damp grass on the soft shoulder of the road, their heads raising up, alerting on the light and noise as the car passed by.

I waited but he didn't say anything.

"Well?"

"Well what?"

"You gonna spill or what?"

"No," he said. "No sir, I is not. But I will tell you two things. One––I don't owe you shit. Two––I'm all in on this thing. Ask me about it again and I'a shoot your ass."

I nodded, not mentioning that was three things.

"Don't think my black ass don't know that was three things," he said.

"You not gonna answer me that, then tell me this."

He slid his hand inside his coat toward the Walther holstered there.

"Don't shoot," I said. "It's a different subject."

"What's that?"

"You never told me."

"What?"

"Were you giving little Clip to Dixon's little Mrs.?"

"Shee-it. Nothin' little about either. Betty Dixon thick as hell––way I like 'em––and if they was anything small about big Clip her husband wouldn't'a wanted to snuff out a nigger's pilot light, would he? 'Sides, you don't believe a brother, all you gots to do is aks your mom."

"Nice."

He smiled.

Mention of Mom reminded me just how long it'd been since I'd spoken to her, and I felt a sharp pang of guilt, but it was short lived, quickly replaced with loss and longing, anger and frustration.

"Much as I like talkin' about thick white women and my big black Clip, how's about you tell me the plan."

"Find her."

He nodded and smiled. "How we gonna do that?"

"Not sure exactly."

"The hell we headed to Tallahassee for?" he said.

I hadn't realized I hadn't told him, and it meant all the more that he was with me, that he was all in without even knowing what in was or where we were headed.

"It's the last place I know for sure she was," I said.

The night Lauren and I had left together, it was to get medical treatment at Johnston's Sanatorium in Tallahassee. After passing out and crashing my car into the main entrance, I had spent two days in a coma and a few more days after that in a drug-induced stupor. When I came out of it, I was told Lauren had been dead on arrival.

"If Harry took her from there and had her pronounced DOA, somebody had to help. Somebody knows something. We're gonna persuade them to tell us what. While we do that, Folsom's searching for De Grasse."

Flaxon De Grasse was a sadistic sex killer who drained all the blood from his bisected victims before displaying them in artistic poses and photographing them. Pale, white, bloodless bodies, black hair on heads and pubes, body parts arranged on a black satin backdrop—a demented surrealist artist creating with actual girls, all of whom, not coincidentally, resembled Lauren. He had yet to be apprehended, and not only did he pose a potential threat to Lauren, he might actually know where she was. He either had something to do with what had happened to her or was connected to those who did.

"There're a few other leads and probably several I haven't thought of," I said, "but these seem—"

I stopped speaking when the patrol lights lit up the inside of our car like a night carnival and the inside of my head with an all too familiar dread.

THE GIRL AT THE END OF THE LONG DARK NIGHT - CHAPTER 2

"Where's the fire, fella?"

The middle-aged man had taken his time walking the short distance from his car to ours, his ambling, awkward movements disjointed in the strobe of the flashing lights.

He was square, flat, and tall, his sheriff's deputy uniform looking like it had been fitted over a thin, wide pine board.

We were idling on the side of Highway 20 next to a pasture, cows close enough to the fence to be seen in the revolving patrol lights and heard over the hum of the engines.

Before I could respond he said, "License and registration, and keep your hands where I can see 'em. Oh, your hand I mean, soldier. Didn't mean any disrespect."

As I slowly and awkwardly used my left to dig the wallet out of my coat pocket, he shone his flashlight beam around the car as best he could, searching the floorboards and backseat before letting it come to rest on Clip.

"Whatta we have here?" he said.

One look at Clip and he straightened up, dropping his hand down near the butt of his revolver and letting it hover there.

"Let me aks you somethin'," Clip said. "I'd'a been drivin', you'd thought I's his chauffeur, wouldn't you?"

"You sassin' me, boy?"

"No suh, not tonight. Tonight I is a seen and not heard house nigger."

The deputy looked confused, but covered it with anger.

"What gives? You boys don't look so good. Y'all got rods under them coats? You look like the sort that would."

Beneath the anger there was a butterfly flutter of nervousness. You could hear it in the subtle tremble at the edge of his voice.

"Sir, I'm Jimmy Riley," I said. "I used to be on the force. I'm a private detective working on an extremely important case. We're in a hurry––"

"No shit you're in a hurry. I mean, hell, soldier, you know you're supposed to keep it under thirty-five. A PI? What's so hell-fire important? Where you headed?"

"Tallahassee. I don't have time to explain. You can radio Panama City PD and talk to Henry Folsom. He'll tell you. We're on the level. I swear it."

"What's his story, your chauffeur? I know he ain't never been no cop. How'd he lose the eye?"

"I training to be a private eye like him," Clip said. "Nobody tol' me you can have two."

"It's my fault," I said. "I should've told him."

"Huh? Oh. A couple of comedians," the cop said. "That's what y'all are. I get it. You've got time to be funny just not to answer my questions, that it?"

"Sorry," I said. "We're so tired we're loopy and we're . . . We meant no harm. Please radio Henry Folsom so we can go."

"So you can go?" he said, his voice rising and filling with humorless amusement. "So what if he says you're who you say you are? So what then? You think you can do what you want in our county 'cause a cop in Panama says you're okay, pal?"

"Then write me a ticket," I said. "Just get on with it."

"Don't know how they do it where you come from, but over here we don't take orders from peepers. No matter how much of a hurry they're in."

"I just meant—"

"I know what you meant, fella, and I don't like it. Not one bit."

"Like I said, we're in a hurry. It's a matter of life and death. We're in search of a missing woman."

"There's blood on your shirt," he said, tension beginning to constrict his voice even more.

"It's mine. My bandage is leaking. I—"

"Step out of the vehicle very slowly," he said. "Both of you. Keep your hands where I can see 'em."

"Listen," I said. "We don't—"

"You listen to me, soldier," he said, removing his revolver from its holster. "I ain't asking and I won't say it again."

We did what he said—me moving first, Clip reluctantly following. When we were out, he motioned us to the back of the car.

"All right, let's have the heaters," he said. "Nice and slow."

I knew Clip wouldn't surrender his under any circumstances. It had gotten me into more than a few jams over the past year or so. No matter the situation. No matter the stakes. Clip would never surrender his weapon. Not ever. And it was going to get us killed.

"Not me," Clip said. "I got mines off a dead man and'll be a dead man 'fore somebody get it off me."

"He means it," I said. "I wish right now he didn't, but I know for a certainty he does."

"Well, I mean to take it, soldier. I'm a man means what he says too. I'm gonna get your gun off you. Even if there's only one way to do it. Ain't no nigger gonna tell me he won't obey a lawful order. No sir."

"Look," I said, reaching into my pocket.

He brought his gun up and pointed it directly at me.

"Here's Henry Folsom's card. How about you call him instead of getting shot."

"I won't be the one to get shot," he said.

"Don't be so sure," Clip said, his Walther pointed at the cop's head.

"What the hell," he said. "How'd you——"

As he started to turn his gun toward Clip, I withdrew mine—— though not as quietly or quickly as Clip had.

"Don't do it," Clip said to him, taking a step toward him and extending his gun another few inches.

The cop stopped in mid turn, his weapon pointed in between us. When he looked back at me, his eyes grew wide to see that I was holding a gun of my own.

"You gettin' better at gettin' that out with your left," Clip said.

"I stay up nights working on it," I said. "Soon all the ladies will call me Quickdraw Riley."

"They say you too quick with somethin', but it ain't you gun."

I returned my attention to the cop.

"We got the drop on you, partner," I said. "Good thing for you we're the good guys——"

"Shee-it," Clip said. "Speak for yourself."

"Good thing for you I'm one of the good guys and mean you no harm. Now, radio Panama City PD. Talk to Folsom and let's all live a little longer. Whatta you say?"

"I ain't puttin' my gun down," he said.

"You will if I tell you to," Clip said. "Ain't no coon ass country motherfucker gonna disobey an unlawful order I give."

"You don't have to," I said.

"Long as you don't point it at me," Clip said.

"Radio Folsom," I said.

He backed toward his car, keeping his gun pointed some- where between us as he did. Standing behind his open door, he reached down into his car, retrieved the mic, and made the call.

The dark December night was cold, the wind a bit biting—causing my every aching cell to ache a little extra.

The flashing lights made me dizzy and the cop difficult to see, and I wondered if he was contemplating shooting at us from the cover of his car.

In the field the cows lowed—mrurr, mrurr, mrurr—and at least one of them had a bell that clanged dully as it moved about.

One shuddered and its muscles could be heard shaking, sounding like the low rumbling of thunder in the distance.

I stepped a few feet closer to the cop and I could hear him talking to Henry Folsom.

When he finished, he tossed the handset back onto the seat of the car, holstered his weapon, and stepped out from behind the door.

"Sorry fellas, but I had to be sure," he said. "You understand. Turns out Captain Folsom's a good friend of Sheriff Tatum. Good luck with finding the—"

Just then his head exploded and he collapsed to the pavement, as other rounds began to ring out and ricochet around us.

THE GIRL AT THE END OF THE LONG DARK NIGHT - CHAPTER 3

With only a split second to determine where the shots were coming from, Clip and I both dove in the ditch behind our car, each of us with our backs against a wheel.

Rounds continued to ricochet around us.

Glass shattered and rained down on the ground. Divots of dirt flew up. Fence posts splintered. Sparks shot up from the pavement.

"How many you figure?" I asked.

"Least two. Too many shots, too fast, too close together to be one. Maybe three. Set up across the street."

The lowing of the cows and the clanging of the bell intensified. Mrurr. Mrurr. Mrurr.

"Keep shooting like this," I said, "they'll be out of ammo soon."

"Lessen they brought a armory wit 'em," Clip said. "Think this got anything to do with us, or just about square pants over there?"

"No way to know for sure, but think if it was just about him, they'd've waited 'til we were gone."

"Lessen they underestimate who he pulled over out here in the middle of nowhere."

We had yet to return fire, waiting for them to run out of rounds or make a move.

Just then a round hit one of the cows and it bellowed loudly as it hit the ground, continuing to moo and moan after it did.

"Motherfuck almighty," Clip said. "Bastards just dropped a cow."

"I saw that."

"May be time for us to start shooting back, they gonna shoot cows and shit."

"Can you see anything?" I asked.

We both turned slightly to get a better view, searching all around us for sight of the shooters.

"Can I see anything," Clip said. "Motherfucker I gots one eye and it ain't all that good."

From beneath the car, I could see the barrel of a rifle in the opposite ditch when the flashing light glinted off it, but that was it.

"Anything?" I said.

"Tol' you I can't see for shit."

He was looking around the back of the car, most of his body still behind the tire.

"Look like one of 'em 'bout to try to sneak up behind the patrol car."

"Got a shot?"

"Will."

"I've got a shooter in the ditch down a little ways. Let's take 'em at the same time. You say when."

I turned and lay facedown on the ground, the cold earth damp and bracing on my body, the pressure on my wound making me wobbly even lying down. Reaching beneath the car, I extended my arm and the revolver as far as I could, using the ground to steady my arm, and thumbed back the hammer.

In the far distance, I could see the first faint hint of headlights approaching from the east.

"Car coming," I said. "Need to go as soon as we can."

"On three," he said.

"Okay."

I waited, but he didn't say anything.

Rounds continue to pock surfaces around us.

Eventually, he said, "One."

I adjusted my grip on the gun. I had never been a great shot and I couldn't shoot for shit with my left, but my left was all I had.

"Two."

Just aim at the barrel. When the balloon goes up, squeeze off five fast rounds.

"Three."

In my periphery, I could see Clip jump up.

We both began firing at nearly the exact same moment.

They fired back at first, then no return fire, then we were out, then nothing.

"Got him," Clip said as he dropped back down behind the car. "You?"

"Can't tell. Be lucky as hell if I did. Was just firing at the glint of a barrel. Never saw anything else."

We waited.

No shots, no bell, just the lowing of the cows, the hum of the motors, and the mechanical whir and tick of the revolving lights.

"Hear that?" Clip asked. "Least they shot the one wearing the bell."

We waited some more.

The lights of the approaching car grew closer and closer until it arrived. It slowed but didn't stop, then sped up, continuing away from us, west, in the direction we had come from.

In another moment, a car about a hundred feet down on the opposite side of the road cranked and raced away east toward

Hosford, its lights only coming on after it was already a piece down the road.

Slowly, cautiously, we came out from behind the car to survey the scene.

We had each gotten our man. Clip's was on the ground behind the patrol car, mine, slumped in the ditch.

"Looks like you got yours," Clip said.

"More likely he shot himself," I said. "Or one of yours ricocheted off your guy and hit him."

"Guess there was a third shooter or a driver waiting in the car. We goin' after him?"

I shook my head. "Gonna radio Folsom. Give him the lay of the land here, then continue on where we were headed."

And after I spoke with Henry Folsom and he agreed to make everything jake with the Liberty County sheriff and clean up our mess, we did.

ALSO BY MICHAEL LISTER

Join Michael's Readers' Group and receive 4 FREE Books!

Books by Michael Lister

Sign up for Michael's newsletter by clicking here or go to
www.MichaelLister.com and receive a free book.

(Jimmy Riley Novels)

The Girl Who Said Goodbye

The Girl in the Grave

The Girl at the End of the Long Dark Night

The Girl Who Cried Blood Tears

The Girl Who Blew Up the World

(John Jordan Novels)

Power in the Blood

Blood of the Lamb

Flesh and Blood

(Special Introduction by Margaret Coel)

The Body and the Blood

Double Exposure

Blood Sacrifice

Rivers to Blood

Burnt Offerings

Innocent Blood

(Special Introduction by Michael Connelly)

Separation Anxiety

Blood Money Blood Moon

Thunder Beach

Blood Cries

A Certain Retribution

Blood Oath

Blood Work

Cold Blood

Blood Betrayal

Blood Shot

Blood Ties

Blood Stone

Blood Trail

(Merrick McKnight / Reggie Summers Novels)

Thunder Beach

A Certain Retribution

Blood Oath

Blood Shot

(Remington James Novels)

Double Exposure

(includes intro by Michael Connelly)

Separation Anxiety

Blood Shot

(Sam Michaels / Daniel Davis Novels)

Burnt Offerings

Blood Oath

Cold Blood

Blood Shot

(Love Stories)

Carrie's Gift

(Short Story Collections)

North Florida Noir

Florida Heat Wave

Delta Blues

Another Quiet Night in Desperation

(The Meaning Series)

Meaning Every Moment

The Meaning of Life in Movies

www.ingramcontent.com/pod-product-compliance
Lightning Source LLC
Chambersburg PA
CBHW021436020726
47499CB00006BA/2022